GALDONI BOOK 3
Out of Darkness
By Cheree L. Alsop

ISBN **149598611x**

Cover Image by Celairen, Mayer George at shutterstock.com and Eric Isselee at shutterstock.com

Cover Design by Andrew Hair

www.chereealsop.com

CHEREE ALSOP

ALSO BY CHEREE ALSOP

The Galdoni Series-
Galdoni
Galdoni 2: Into the Storm
Galdoni 3: Out of Darkness
Galdoni 4

The Silver Series-
Silver
Black
Crimson
Violet
Azure
Hunter
Silver Moon

The Small Town Superheroes Series-
Small Town Superhero
Small Town Superhero II
Small Town Superhero III

Heart of the Wolf Part One
Heart of the Wolf Part Two
Keeper of the Wolves
Stolen
The Million Dollar Gift
Thief Prince
Shadows
Mist

3

PRAISE FOR CHEREE ALSOP

The Galdoni Series

"This is absolutely one of the best books I have ever read in my life! I loved the characters and their personalities, the storyline and the way it was written. The bravery, courage and sacrifice that Kale showed was amazing and had me scolding myself to get a grip and stop crying! This book had adventure, romance and comedy all rolled into one terrific book I LOVED the lesson in this book, the struggles that the characters had to go through (especially the forbidden love)...I couldn't help wondering what it would be like to live among such strangely beautiful creatures that acted, at times, more caring and compassionate than the humans. Overall, I loved this book...I recommend it to ANYONE who fancies great books."
—iBook Reviewer

"I was pleasantly surprised by this book! The characters were so well written as if the words themselves became life. The sweet romance between hero and heroine made me root for the underdog more than I usually do! I definitely recommend this book!"
—Sara Phillipp

"Can't wait for the next book!! Original idea and great characters. Could not put the book down; read it in one sitting."
—StanlyDoo- Amazon Reviewer

"5 stars! Amazing read. The story was great- the plot flowed and kept throwing the unexpected at you. Wonderfully established setting in place; great character development, shown very well thru well placed dialogue- which in turn kept the story moving right along! No bog downs or boring parts in this book! Loved the originality that stemmed from ancient mysticism- bringing age old fiction into modern day reality. Recommend for teenage and older- action violence a little intense for preteen years, but overall this is a great action thriller slash mini romance novel."

—That Lisa Girl, Amazon Reviewer

"I was not expecting a free novel to beat anything that I have ever laid eyes upon. This book was touching and made me want more after each sentence."

—Sears1994, iBook Reviewer

"This book was simply heart wrenching. It was an amazing book with a great plot. I almost cried several times. All of the scenes were so real it felt like I was there witnessing everything."

—Jeanine Drake, iBook Reveiwer

"This book was absolutely amazing...It had me tearing at parts, cursing at others, and filled with adrenaline rushing along with the characters at the fights. It is a book for everyone, with themes of love, courage, hardship, good versus evil, humane and inhumane...All around, it is an amazing book!"

—Mkb312, iBook Reviewer

"Galdoni is an amazing book; it is the first to actually make me cry! It is a book that really touches your heart, a

romance novel that might change the way you look at someone. It did that to me."
—Coralee2, Reviewer

"Wow. I simply have no words for this. I highly recommend it to anyone who stumbled across this masterpiece. In other words, READ IT!"
—Troublecat101, iBook Reviewer

The Silver Series

"Cheree Alsop has written *Silver* for the YA reader who enjoys both werewolves and coming-of-age tales. Although I don't fall into this demographic, I still found it an entertaining read on a long plane trip! The author has put a great deal of thought into balancing a tale that could apply to any teen (death of a parent, new school, trying to find one's place in the world) with the added spice of a youngster dealing with being exceptionally different from those around him, and knowing that puts him in danger."
—Robin Hobb, author of the Farseer Trilogy

"I honestly am amazed this isn't absolutely EVERYWHERE! Amazing book. Could NOT put it down! After reading this book, I purchased the entire series!"
—Josephine, Amazon Reviewer

"Great book, Cheree Alsop! The best of this kind I have read in a long time. I just hope there is more like this one."
—Tony Olsen

"I couldn't put the book down. I fell in love with the characters and how wonderfully they were written. Can't wait to read the 2nd!"
—Mary A. F. Hamilton

"A page-turner that kept me wide awake and wanting more. Great characters, well written, tenderly developed, and thrilling. I loved this book, and you will too."
—Valerie McGilvrey

"Super glad that I found this series! I am crushed that it is at its end. I am sure we will see some of the characters in the next series, but it just won't be the same. I am 41 years old, and am only a little embarrassed to say I was crying at 3 a.m. this morning while finishing the last book. Although this is a YA series, all ages will enjoy the Silver Series. Great job by Cheree Alsop. I am excited to see what she comes up with next."
—Jennc, Amazon Reviewer

Keeper of the Wolves

"This is without a doubt the VERY BEST paranormal romance/adventure I have ever read and I've been reading these types of books for over 45 years. Excellent plot, wonderful protagonists—even the evil villains were great. I read this in one sitting on a Saturday morning when there were so many other things I should have been doing. I COULD NOT put it down! I also appreciated the author's research and insights into the behavior of wolf packs. I will

CERTAINLY read more by this author and put her on my 'favorites' list."
—N. Darisse

"This is a novel that will emotionally cripple you. Be sure to keep a box of tissues by your side. You will laugh, you will cry, and you will fall in love with Keeper. If you loved *Black Beauty* as a child, then you will truly love *Keeper of the Wolves* as an adult. Put this on your 'must read' list."
—Fortune Ringquist

"Cheree Alsop mastered the mind of a wolf and wrote the most amazing story I've read this year. Once I started, I couldn't stop reading. Personal needs no longer existed. I turned the last page with tears streaming down my face."
—Rachel Andersen, Amazon Reviewer

"I truly enjoyed this book very much. I've spent most of my life reading supernatural books, but this was the first time I've read one written in first person and done so well. I must admit that the last half of this book had me in tears from sorrow and pain for the main character and his dilemma as a man and an animal. . . Suffice it to say that this is one book you REALLY need in your library. I won't ever regret purchasing this book, EVER! It was just that GOOD! I would also recommend you have a big box of tissues handy because you WILL NEED THEM! Get going, get the book..."
—Kathy I, Amazon Reviewer

"I just finished this book. Oh my goodness, did I get emotional in some spots. It was so good. The courage and love portrayed is amazing. I do recommend this book. Thought provoking."

—Candy, Amazon Reviewer

Thief Prince

"I absolutely loved this book! I could not put it down. . . The Thief Prince will whisk you away into a new world that you will not want to leave! I hope that Ms. Alsop has more about this story to write, because I would love more Kit and Andric! This is one of my favorite books so far this year! Five Stars!"

—Crystal, Book Blogger at Books are Sanity

". . . Once I started I couldn't put it down. The story is amazing. The plot is new and the action never stops. The characters are believable and the emotions presented are beautiful and real. If anyone wants a good, clean, fun, romantic read, look no further. I hope there will be more books set in Debria, or better yet, Antor."

—SH Writer, Amazon Reviewer

"This book was a roller coaster of emotions: tears, laughter, anger, and happiness. I absolutely fell in love with all of the characters placed throughout this story. This author knows how to paint a picture with words."

—Kathleen Vales

"Awesome book! It was so action packed, I could not put it down, and it left me wanting more! It was very well written, leaving me feeling like I had a connection with the characters."

—M. A., Amazon Reviewer

"I am a Cheree Alsop junkie and I have to admit, hands down, this is my FAVORITE of anything she has published. In a world separated by race, fear and power are forced to collide in order to save them all. Who better to free them of the prejudice than the loyal heart of a Duskie? Adventure, incredible amounts of imagination, and description go into this world! It is a 'buy now and don't leave the couch until the last chapter has reached an end' kind of read!"

—Malcay, Amazon Reviewer

"I absolutely loved this book! I could not put it down! Anything with a prince and a princess is usually a winner for me, but this book is even better! It has multiple princes and princesses on scene over the course of the book! I was completely drawn into Kit's world as she was faced with danger and new circumstances...Kit was a strong character, not a weak and simpering girl who couldn't do anything for herself. The Thief Prince (Andric) was a great character as well! I kept seeing glimpses of who he really was and I loved that the author gave us clues as to what he was like under the surface. The Thief Prince will whisk you away into a new world that you will not want to leave!"

—Bookworm, Book Reviewer

Small Town Superhero Series

"A very human superhero- Cheree Alsop has written a great book for youth and adults alike. Kelson, the superhero, is battling his own demons plus bullies in this action packed narrative. Small Town Superhero had me from the first sentence through the end. I felt every sorrow, every pain and the delight of rushing through the dark on a motorcycle. Descriptions in Small Town Superhero are so well written the reader is immersed in the town and lives of its inhabitants."

—Rachel Andersen, Book Reviewer

"Anyone who grew up in a small town or around motorcycles will love this! It has great characters and flows well with martial arts fighting and conflicts involved."

—Karen, Amazon Reviewer

"Fantastic story...and I love motorcycles and heroes who don't like the limelight. Excellent character development. You'll like this series!"

—Michael, Amazon Reviewer

"Another great read; couldn't put it down. Would definitely recommend this book to friends and family. She has put out another great read. Looking forward to reading more!"

—Benton Garrison, Amazon Reviewer

"I enjoyed this book a lot. Good teen reading. Most books I read are adult contemporary; I needed a change and this was a good change. I do recommend reading this book! I will be looking out for more books from this author. Thank you!"

—Cass, Amazon Reviewer

Stolen

"This book will take your heart, make it a little bit bigger, and then fill it with love. I would recommend this book to anyone from 10-100. To put this book in words is like trying to describe love. I had just gotten it and I finished it the next day because I couldn't put it down. If you like action, thrilling fights, and/or romance, then this is the perfect book for you."

—Steven L. Jagerhorn

"Couldn't put this one down! Love Cheree's ability to create totally relatable characters and a story told so fluidly you actually believe it's real."

—Sue McMillin, Amazon Reviewer

"I enjoyed this book it was exciting and kept you interested. The characters were believable. And the teen romance was cute."

—Book Haven- Amazon Reviewer

"This book written by Cheree Alsop was written very well. It is set in the future and what it would be like for government control. The drama was great and the story was very well put together. If you want something different, then this is the book to get and it is a page turner for sure. You will love the main characters as well, and the events that unfold during the story. It will leave you hanging and wanting more."

—Kathy Hallettsville, TX- Amazon Reviewer

"I really liked this book . . . I was pleasantly surprised to discover this well-written book. . .I'm looking forward to reading more from this author."

—Julie M. Peterson- Amazon Reviewer

"Great book! I enjoyed this book very much it keeps you wanting to know more! I couldn't put it down! Great read!"

—Meghan- Amazon Reviewer

"A great read with believable characters that hook you instantly. . . I was left wanting to read more when the book was finished."

—Katie- Goodreads Reviewer

Heart of the Wolf

"Absolutely breathtaking! This book is a roller coaster of emotions that will leave you exhausted!!! A beautiful fantasy filled with action and love. I recommend this book to all fantasy lovers and those who enjoy a heartbreaking love story that rivals that of Romeo and Juliet. I couldn't put this book down!"

—Amy May

"What an awesome book! A continual adventure, with surprises on every page. What a gifted author she is. You just can't put the book down. I read it in two days. Cheree has a way of developing relationships and pulling at your heart. You find yourself identifying with the characters in her book...True life situations make this book come alive for you and gives you increased understanding of your own situation in life. Magnificent story and characters. I've read all of

Cheree's books and recommend them all to you...especially if you love adventures."
—Michael, Amazon Reviewer

"You'll like this one and want to start part two as soon as you can! If you are in the mood for an adventure book in a faraway kingdom where there are rival kingdoms plotting and scheming to gain more power, you'll enjoy this novel. The characters are well developed, and of course with Cheree there is always a unique supernatural twist thrown into the story as well as romantic interests to make the pages fly by."
Karen, Amazon Reviewer

When Death Loved an Angel

"This style of book is quite a change for this author so I wasn't expecting this, but I found an interesting story of two very different souls who stepped outside of their "accepted roles" to find love and forgiveness, and what is truly of value in life and death."
—Karen, Amazon Reviewer

"When Death Loved an Angel by Cheree Alsop is a touching paranormal romance that cranks the readers' thinking mode into high gear."
—Rachel Andersen, Book Reviewer

"Loved this book. I would recommend this book to everyone. And be sure to check out the rest of her books, too!"
—Malcay, Book Reviewer

The Shadows Series

". . . This author has talent. I enjoyed her world, her very well developed characters, and an interesting, entertaining concept and story. Her introduction to her world was well done and concise. . . .Her characters were interesting enough that I became attached to several. I would certainly read a follow-up if only to check on the progress and evolution of the society she created. I recommend this for any age other than those overly sensitive to some graphic violence. The romance was heartfelt but pg. A good read."
—Mari, Amazon Reviewer

". . . I've fallen for the characters and their world. I've even gone on to share (this book) with my sister. . .So many moments made me smile as well as several which brought tears from the attachment; not sad tears, I might add. When I started Shadows, I didn't expect much because I assumed it was like most of the books I've read lately. But this book was one of the few books to make me happy I was wrong and find myself so far into the books that I lost track of time, ending up reading to the point that my body said I was too tired to continue reading! I can't wait to see what happens in the next book. . . Some of my new favorite quotes will be coming from this lovely novel. Thank you to Cheree Alsop for allowing the budding thoughts to come to life. I am a very hooked reader."
—Stephanie Roberts, Amazon Reviewer

"This was a heart-warming tale of rags to riches. It was also wonderfully described and the characters were vivid and vibrant; a story that teaches of love defying boundaries and of people finding acceptance."

—Sara Phillip, Book Reviewer

"This is the best book I have ever had the pleasure of reading. . . It literally has everything, drama, action, fighting, romance, adventure, & suspense. . . Nexa is one of the most incredible female protagonists ever written. . .It literally had me on pins & needles the ENTIRE time. . . I cannot recommend this book highly enough. Please give yourself a wonderful treat & read this book... you will NOT be disappointed!!!"
—Jess- Goodreads Reviewer

"Took my breath away; excitement, adventure and suspense. . . This author has extracted a tender subject and created a supernatural fantasy about seeing beyond the surface of an individual. . . Also the romantic scenes would make a girl swoon. . . The fights between allies and foes and blood lust would attract the male readers. . .The conclusion was so powerful and scary this reader was sitting on the edge of her seat."
—Susan Mahoney, Book Blogger

"Adventure, incredible amounts of imagination and description go into this world! It is a buy now, don't leave the couch until the last chapter has reached an end kind of read!"
—Malcay- Amazon Reviewer

"The high action tale with the underlying love story that unfolds makes you want to keep reading and not put it down. I can't wait until the next book in the Shadows Series comes out."
—Karen- Amazon Reviewer

CHEREE ALSOP

"Really enjoyed this book. A modern fairy tale complete with Kings and Queens, Princesses and Princes, castles and the damsel is not quite in distress. LOVE IT."
—Braine, Talk Supe- Book Blogger

". . . It's refreshing to see a female character portrayed without the girly cliches most writers fall into. She is someone I would like to meet in real life, and it is nice to read the first person POV of a character who is so well-round that she is brave, but still has the softer feminine side that defines her character. A definite must read."
—S. Teppen- Goodreads Reviewer

"I really enjoyed this book and had a hard time putting it down. . . This premise is interesting and the world building was intriguing. The author infused the tale with the feeling of suspicion and fear . . . The author does a great job with characterization and you grow to really feel for the characters throughout especially as they change and begin to see Nexa's point of view. . . I did enjoy the book and the originality. I would recommend this for young adult fantasy lovers. It's more of a mild dark fantasy, but it would definitely fall more in the traditional fantasy genre . "
—Jill- Goodreads Reviewer

To my husband who is my sun,
My moon, and my stars.
To my children for bringing
Light wherever they go.
I love your laughter,
Your smiles, and the joy
That fills every day.

Chapter One

I tipped my wings into the wind and smiled when it drove me higher through the clouds. Lost amid the white fog, I could pretend that nothing existed below. I loved the wind. I closed my eyes and let it push me at its whim. The wind had so many different temperaments. It could fight like the fiercest warrior, whisper its tantalizing thoughts of freedom, or make grown men seek shelter against its rage. The wind could make its way through the smallest crack or cause the tallest building to groan with its force. I wanted to be the wind.

My location nudged at the back of my thoughts. I sighed. Despite the clouds, I could feel that I was close to the school. The animal side of me rebelled at being a prisoner inside its impassive gray walls, while the Galdoni side flooded me with memories of the Academy. Regardless of my trepidation, I had to go.

I gritted my teeth and pulled my wings tight against my back, slicing through the cloud cover. A building loomed inches to my right, so close that the blue feathers of my wing brushed it. I used my wings to turn me just enough that I cleared the buildings. At the last second, I spread them. The force jerked me back. I landed with a grin on the empty street.

The grin faded when I saw where I was. Because of the drug-free zone, the school boundaries started at the edge of the block where I stood. It was the no-fly zone, thanks to the Galdoni integration laws. Though it was unlawful for a Galdoni student to hide their wings from view with a coat or other clothing, we were unable to use them on school property. The irony never failed to frustrate me. I couldn't decide if it was to protect the students or continually remind them of how different I was. It felt like the same thing to me.

The sound of voices deepened my trepidation. I could have landed on the other side of the school. It would have been easier. Yet I was a Galdoni. I didn't avoid a fight even if I wasn't allowed to participate in it.

"Nice of you to join us, cur," Brayce said in a forced pleasant tone.

I lifted my lips in more of a snarl than a smile.

"Get it, cur," Tavin, once of Brayce's cronies, piped in. "It means mixed-breed mongrel. So it's like you, because you're part animal, part human, like, well, a cur!"

"Shut up, Tavin," Brayce snapped.

Tavin closed his mouth, but continued to bounce from one foot to the other. In all the time I've known the kid, he had never been able to hold still. The prospects of a fight made it worse. His parents should probably get him looked at.

"How long did you spend reading the dictionary to come up with that one, Brayce?" I asked, keeping my tone light.

"Long enough to know they still haven't classified Galdoni as a member of the human race," Brayce replied, his dark eyes glittering at the sore spot. "So really, you're just an animal allowed to go to school, like a service pet."

"Whose service is to tear off your arms and shove them down your throat," I replied, unable to keep my composure any longer.

Brayce's hands clenched. He walked close enough that I had to back up to keep from letting his nose touch mine. "You think you're so tough?" he growled, his face inches away.

Spit hit my cheek. He flinched when I lifted a hand to wipe it away; the small token of his fear gave me brief satisfaction. "I think you have bad breath," I replied.

Tavin and Manny, Tavin's twin, snickered. Brayce glared at them and they stopped. He leaned closer to me. "You don't deserve to be here, cur. You're nothing but a talking animal playing circus to the amusement of the school board." He lifted his hands, beckoning me on. "Come on, mongrel. One punch. That's all I need."

One punch and I would be permanently expelled from high school. The Galdoni integration laws were extremely unforgiving on that point. Kale had seen to it that I knew the consequences of such an action. One punch and I could ruin it for all Galdoni.

"Are you afraid?" Brayce pressed. He threw a punch at my face.

I ducked and had to fight back the impulse to answer it with one of my own in his ample gut.

"Don't be a coward," Brayce continued. He tipped his head at Chad, the last member of his gang who stood with his hands in his pockets and his back against the far wall. Chad was a few years older than the average high school student; his answers in class let me know that academics weren't his strong point. The boy's eyes carried no emotion as he crossed to Brayce's side. It was like looking at a shark. His shaved head and stocky build added to the impression.

"Hit him, Chad!" Tavin said, bouncing up and down.

"Make him bleed," Manny encouraged, his fists clenched and excitement on his face despite the fact that I could snap the beanpole kid in two. He kept his distance for a very good reason.

When Chad swung, I dodged to the left. His fist slammed into the brick wall behind me. A roar of rage left the boy's mouth. Brayce tried to kick me in the stomach. I caught his leg and used his body to block Chad's angry bull rush. Both students fell against the wall. They charged me with fists flying. I blocked three punches. The next grazed my cheekbone. I blocked a kick with my forearms and fought the impulse to slug Chad in the groin.

I ducked under a haymaker, grabbed Brayce's arm, and used his momentum to send him into Chad. Both charged me. I caught one of Chad's hammer punches with a forearm, but paid for it when Brayce's fist caught me in the ribs. I knocked aside his chop aimed at my throat. I was about to block Chad's fist in the ribs again when Brayce landed a knee to my groin. Red flared in my vision. My hands clenched. I brought a fist back, intent on laying Brayce out on the ground.

"What's going on here?"

Saro's voice deflated my rage as quickly as if he had thrown ice cold water in my face. I blinked and focused on the gold-winged Galdoni who had just landed at the mouth of the alley. He looked from me to Brayce's gang. The line of his jaw was tight despite his pleasant tone as if he was fully aware of what he had just interrupted.

"N-nothing, sir," Brayce stuttered.

Tavin and Manny were already running down the alley toward the school.

Chad held up his hands and backed away, still with the emotionless expression in his eyes.

"Shouldn't you guys be in class?" Saro suggested.

"Y-yes, sir," Brayce agreed. He picked up his backpack and glanced at Chad. The pair jogged down the alley after Tavin and Manny.

"What was that?" Saro asked quietly when they were out of earshot.

"Nothing I couldn't handle," I replied, willing my muscles to relax.

"It looked to me like you were ready to tear off his legs and beat him with them."

I couldn't suppress a chuckle. "It had crossed my mind."

Saro nodded. "Do I need to remind you that we're walking a fine line here?"

I shook my head, frustration filling my chest. "No. It just doesn't seem right that they can do whatever they want and at the first punch, I'm the one expelled."

Saro cracked a smile. "That's because your first punch will be their last."

I shrugged. "It only takes one to remind them."

"And then they're dead."

"One less Galdoni problem," I said with an edge of hopefulness.

Saro let out a breath. "You know that's not how it works."

"What if I ask Kale to let Goliath give me defensive combat training so that I can hone my skill in avoiding punches?"

Saro shook his head. "You know the rules, Reece."

I kicked at a clump of debris that turned out to be a half-eaten apple covered in dirt. It squished when my shoe made contact. I scraped the toe of my sneaker on the cement to clean it off. "I know. Galdoni integration rules deny Galdoni students from training for fear that it will increase our aggression and lead to more fights with the human students."

"I know it's hard."

I would have argued the point, but I knew it was true. Saro had been my mentor since I started at Crosby High. He had never hidden his history from me. I knew how hard he had fought to live a life of peace. The blood on his hands sometimes showed in his eyes when he didn't think anyone was looking. Regrets hung on his shoulders, but he carried them without complaint. I respected him for that.

"What if I drop out?" I asked, testing the waters. At his surprised look, I rushed on, "Then you wouldn't need to worry about me messing up."

"You can't drop out," he said. "You're sixteen. You should be in school."

"Skylar did, and she's fine," I pointed out.

"She'd be graduated by now, and she had to do it to support her family. She would have rather been in school, trust me," Saro replied.

"I can support the Galdoni. I'll get a job."

"Doing what?"

I smirked. "Delivery boy. Think of how fast the pizza could get to someone's house? I could make records."

Saro grinned at me. "That's for sure." The bell rang in the distance. "You better get going."

I sighed. "Fine, but pizza sounds good right about now."

"Go," Saro urged with a laugh.

I waved at him and jogged up the alley where Brayce's gang had gone. At least I didn't have to worry about them jumping me before I got to the doors. They were too afraid of Saro for that; but I knew I would pay for his interference.

I pushed the set of double doors open.

"You're late!" Seth's always present smile lit his wide cheeks. He held out my algebra book. "I almost thought you weren't coming, but that wouldn't be like you. I had to hide when Brayce's bouncers came through, so I figured they were the reason you were delayed." He looked at me, expecting an answer. He always spoke in a rush when he was excited or nervous.

24

"You know hanging out with me keeps you on their radar," I pointed out for the hundredth time.

Seth shrugged. "It's worth a trashcan or two to hang out with a Galdoni."

The reverence with which he said Galdoni made it sound like I was a hero or something. I snorted and took the math book he held out. "You know you don't have to go to my locker."

He grinned. "I like to help." His red hair stuck up at the front of his head, something he was constantly trying to smooth down. He patted it with one hand, but to no avail. The cowlick refused to obey.

I walked down the hall toward our classroom and he chatted happily at my side. "I did some research into the color of birds' wings, more specifically, the Bluejay and Indigo Bunting. Did you know that your wings are blue only because your feathers have barbs with cells filled with air that scatter the blue light and trap the red wavelengths? Your feathers would actually be black if it wasn't for that!"

I nodded, because he expected it. I was so used to his ramblings that I rarely bothered with paying strict attention to them anymore. He was generally just happy talking when there was someone listening.

"On a secondary note, did you know that the Galdoni with white wings have weaker feathers and if they ate carotenoids, their feathers could turn pink like a flamingo's?"

I paused and glanced at him. "Where could I get carotenoids?"

His eyebrows rose as if he was surprised I had actually been listening. "Well, flamingos eat algae and other organisms that are high in alpha and beta carotenoid pigments from the mud at the bottom of shallow pools. Maybe we could get some of that?"

"I'm not sure I'd be able to sneak mud into their meals at the Center. We may have to look for other options."

Seth laughed. He pulled open the door to algebra. "See you at gym!"

All heads in the classroom turned in our direction. Seth's face blushed as red as his hair. "Uh, sorry about that," he whispered. He pushed his backpack strap higher onto his shoulder and ran down the hall at breakneck speed toward his English class.

"Thank you for joining us, Reece," Mr. Bennett said in a dry tone.

I ignored his eye roll and made my way down the middle row. My seat was at the back, which usually appealed to me, except it meant walking past classmates who didn't take kindly to my presence.

That fact was emphasized when someone yanked out one of my feathers. I spun, ready to take them down as my instincts commanded.

"Something wrong, Reece?" Mr. Bennett asked. His usually monotone voice contained a hint of warning.

I let out a slow breath to calm my pounding heart. My eyes searched the hands of the students around me. Nobody met my gaze. A few had apologetic looks on their faces as if sorry the game had gotten out of hand, yet the blue feather was nowhere to be seen.

"Everything's fine, Mr. Bennett," I replied tightly. I let my textbook fall with a bang loud enough to cause several students to jump before I slid onto the hard seat.

Chapter Two

I turned my attention to the window as I did every day during class. It was the only way to stay sane.

The black birds sat on the telephone wire as they always did. I could almost hear their chattering through the window. A few more birds landed. Disgruntled at the suddenly cramped space, a bird in the middle took flight.

I watched him soar over the trees that lined the school's soccer field. He pushed his wings hard, flapping so that he rose above the stands before catching the breeze. His wings opened wide, feathers lifting as they filled with the wind, the fickle, carefree wind nobody could control. It had a mind of its own; nobody trapped it in a box or told it to be something it wasn't. It wouldn't listen anyway.

"Reece?"

Giggles brought me back to the present.

"Don't mind him," Dennis said from the front row. "He's out there with the birds where he belongs."

"I'll have none of that talk in my classroom." Mr. Bennett snapped. His eyes flashed behind his glasses. The student's comment had angered the teacher even more than me. He met Dennis' gaze. "I'll see you for detention after school."

"Why?" Dennis asked, appalled. "What did I do?"

"Prejudice isn't acceptable, Mr. Hansen. If you choose to be made an example of, then I must follow through," Mr. Bennett answered.

Dennis slammed his algebra book shut and crossed his arms to stare moodily at the wall.

Mr. Bennett ignored him. "I asked if you have the answer to the problem, Reece."

I studied the numbers on the board. Luckily, I had been taught math since I could walk. Numbers were easy; they didn't care who you were or where you fit into the scheme of things. As long as you lined them up right, they would always fall into place.

"A is negative three over five and B is thirteen fifths," I answered.

Mr. Bennett looked from me to the board. "Did you write that down?" he asked.

I shook my head. "Lucky guess."

A hint of a smile showed on his lips before he turned back to the board. "Reece is right." He proceeded to write out the formula to solve the equation.

I was about to look back out the window when the door opened. As with my entrance, all eyes turned to see who it was. My heart skipped a complete beat, the kind that steals the breath from your lungs for a minute until you remember that you have to take in air again.

She was beautiful. Her long black hair was pulled back on one side by a clip with an emerald in the middle. The jewel matched the exact color of her eyes, which creased at the corners as though she smiled often as she handed Mr. Bennett her enrollment slip. She wore a blue cardigan over a lacy cream-colored shirt that accentuated the dark gray feathers of the wings that rose from her back.

"Pleased to meet you, Ms. Ava," Mr. Bennett said, glancing at her paper. "I'll have to get you a chair. We're out of desks at the moment, but I'll make sure one is brought before tomorrow."

"I'm sorry for the inconvenience," she apologized.

There was a sweetness to her voice that made me smile. I smothered the feeling and glared at my desk.

"No inconvenience," Mr. Bennett hurried to point out. "I'll be happy to make sure it is done. For now, here is an extra textbook." He grabbed one from the bookshelf beside

28

his desk. He glanced at it, and his face turned red. A few students laughed. He had made a big deal about showing the same book to the class the day before, careful to block out what he could of the foul language sprawled across the front in big black letters. "I-I apologize, Ms. Ava. This book is inappropriate. I'll have to find you another of those as well."

"Thank you," she replied.

Her smile seemed to have a calming effect on the teacher. He smoothed his tie and showed her to her seat before he hurried back to the front. No one heard anything else from his lecture.

If I attracted trouble and repelled kindness like a duck in water, Ava was the complete opposite. Where my wings had given the students plenty of reasons to shun me, Ava garnered attention from every corner.

"Your feathers are so beautiful; can I touch them?" Alice, the head cheerleader, asked.

"What products do you use in your hair?" Amelia, Alice's second in command and constant shadow, pressed.

"Did you fly or take a bus?" a boy with a ring through his eyebrow asked.

Melody, the girl who on occasion went so far as to smile at me, leaned toward Ava. "I didn't know we would get a female Galdoni here!" she exclaimed.

Mr. Bennett continued with the lesson the best he could despite the loud conversation on the right side of the room. He shot glances that way, but apparently he was glad to see everyone getting along and felt it would be better to lecture no one than to interrupt.

Ava fielded questions politely as if she was used to being besieged by curious students. She glanced my way once. I felt her eyes on my wings before she met my gaze, her expression curious. I turned back to the window and focused my attention on the birds once more despite the fact that I very much wanted only to watch her. She had a way of speaking and smiling as if every person she talked to was the very person she had been wanting to converse with. By the time the bell rang, students on the left side of the room had moved to the right, crowding the desks. Mr. Bennett eventually gave up, but nobody noticed.

Ava rose. "I guess I should find my next class."

"Where is it?"

"What are you taking?"

Other offers to help her find her way sounded from the students around her. Ava smiled and handed her paper to Alice. The head cheerleader nodded as though the action was expected; she read through the schedule swiftly.

"You have economics next, and then choir." She flicked a ringlet of her long red hair back behind her shoulder with one annoyed finger. "We'll be back together in English. I'll make sure Mrs. Simmons assigns you a seat next to me."

"Thank you," Ava said.

"I have economics next," the boy with the ring through his eyebrow said.

Alice's gaze flicked past him. "Jeffrey, you'll take her to Mr. Durmont's, won't you?"

"Of course," the football player replied. He held out his elbow to Ava. She glanced at it uncertainly as if unsure what to do with it. I smothered a smile as I picked up my book. Jeffrey shrugged and accepted the schedule from Alice. After some jostling for space and positions, all the students crowded out the door together.

I crossed the empty room to the door.

"Have a good day, Reece," Mr. Bennett said.

I paused. It was the first time he had ever gone out of his way to say something to me besides pointing out my lateness. "I, uh, thank you, Mr. Bennett," I replied.

He rubbed his eyes beneath his glasses; he already looked tired and the day had just started. "You know you should probably be in an advanced placement class, right?"

I nodded. "It's nice to have one easy class here."

He chuckled, smiling for the first time I had ever seen. "I don't think your fellow students would agree."

I dropped my gaze. "If you haven't noticed, they're not exactly my fellow students."

I left through the door before he could reply.

"Good thing your guardian showed up to protect you out there," Brayce's grating voice met me when I entered the hallway.

"Yeah, good thing your guardian showed up," Tavin echoed.

"I thought you were going to cry," Brayce pressed, crossing the hall to confront me. The boy had serious boundary issues. He stopped so close I was forced to duck to the side to get around him. He followed me and said, "I thought Galdoni were big and tough. You're nothing but a coward, cur."

My control snapped. I grabbed Brayce by the throat and slammed him against a locker. His feet kicked in the air as he struggled to get free. Manny and Tavin stared. I wondered where Chad was. My instincts warned me to be on lookout for a surprise attack. Perhaps the taunting had been a trap. My grip tightened.

"Reece."

Mr. Bennett's voice broke me from the haze. I blinked at Brayce, willing my gaze to clear. His eyes were bulging as he clawed at my hand. I loosened my grip and let him fall to the floor. Tavin and Manny helped him up. I watched them struggle down the hallway with Brayce leaning heavily on their shoulders before I glanced at Mr. Bennett.

"I don't want to see you expelled," he said.

I rubbed the back of my neck, willing the adrenaline to fade from my thundering heart. "I'm getting closer to it," I admitted.

Mr. Bennett's eyebrows pulled together. "Bullies have been around since time began," he said. "We all have to learn to deal with them one way or another."

I touched the locker where Brayce's head had given it a slight dent. "The problem comes when the victim can kill the bully if he loses control."

Mr. Bennett tipped his head slightly to one side. "I've never thought of a Galdoni as a victim."

I smiled despite my frustration. "We're not. I'm worried Brayce is going to learn that sooner rather than later."

Mr. Bennett leaned against the lockers across the hall. "Maybe what you're here to learn is how to keep your cool in stressful situations."

I nodded. "It's definitely not gym." At his look, I explained, "Climbing the rope seems a bit pointless when you have wings."

He smiled. "I suppose it would be. Maybe down the road they'll take that into consideration."

"If I don't get the whole Galdoni integration revoked."

Mr. Bennett shrugged. "They had to start somewhere."

I studied the locker next to him. Someone had scratched the initials X.J. into the red paint. "I just hope the Galdoni at other schools are doing better than I am."

Mr. Bennett nodded. He pushed off the locker and headed back toward his classroom. Students began to file in. I headed down the hall.

"Reece?"

I turned.

Mr. Bennett had paused by his door. "You know, sometime everyone is going to have to accept the fact that you're just another student here, even you."

The thought made me smile. "Let's hope it comes to that."

He nodded and waved me away.

Chapter Three

"See you tomorrow," Seth said. He grinned. "It'll be another awesome day!"

I smiled. "I don't know how you keep it up."

"What?" he asked.

I waved a hand vaguely at the crowded hallway. "Staying so cheerful amid all of this."

He shrugged, leaning against the locker next to my open one. "Since you got here, Brayce's bouncers pick on me only half as much. That's a good thing."

I shoved him amiably.

He laughed, then tripped and stumbled into a gaggle of girls. One of them, a girl with brown hair in two braids, dropped her books.

"My poetry!" she exclaimed, kneeling on the floor to pick up the sheets of paper that flew everywhere.

"I-I'm so sorry," Seth stuttered. He dropped to his knees to help her.

I took pity on him and joined the frantic gathering of papers and books before the indifferent crowd destroyed all of her work completely.

"I'm so sorry," Seth kept repeating. "I didn't mean to, really. I would never bump you like that on purpose."

"I know, Seth. It's okay," she replied, rising to her feet as she tried to get the papers into some semblance of order.

Seth froze, his eyes on her and the papers motionless in his hands. "You-you know my name?" he asked in surprise.

"Of course," she replied. "You're friends with the—"

I held out several papers and her eyes flew to me. Her cheeks turned red. She dropped her gaze and took the papers. "Thank you," she said quietly.

I shut my locker and left Seth gathering up the rest of the papers with the girl. I passed Ava in the front office. She was chatting with Mrs. Jeffrey while she filled out a form I assumed was for enrollment. I pushed open the front door and made my way down the sidewalk.

It looked like I might actually make it past the school property line unprovoked. I almost started jogging at the sight of the end of the block. The way the buildings loomed, it looked almost as if daylight started there because the sun basked the sidewalk just past the buildings in warm light. A smile spread across my face at the thought of flying.

Something hit me in the back of the head. I turned. My heart slowed at the sight of a dozen students following Brayce. I recognized them as the most Galdoni unfriendly at the school. Brayce had been busy.

"You think it's funny to pick on unarmed students?" Brayce asked, his tone taunting. His throat was still red from our little scuffle earlier. He apparently wasn't ready to let it go.

I raised my hands. "I don't want to fight you, Brayce," I said in as calm a tone as I could muster.

Freedom was feet away. I could run for the boundary and fly off. I could leave Brayce and his bullies behind to deal with another day. The thought was very appealing; too bad I wasn't a coward.

"You confused me with the way you attacked me at school today," Brayce replied. He glanced back at the students behind him. By the looks on their faces, they had been told a very skewed story of what had happened.

"There's laws against you fighting students," someone called out.

"You could have killed him," another shouted.

"You shouldn't even be here," a girl echoed.

"See," Brayce said with a shrug. "Apparently I'm not the only one who doesn't like you."

"I don't need anyone to like me," I replied.

He held something up in his right hand. I realized it was the feather someone had pulled from my wing during algebra. He flicked a lighter in his left hand and put it to the feather. The brilliant blue feather shriveled as it burned. It lent an acrid scent to the air.

"Look at that," Brayce said. "Curs can burn."

"Curs can burn!" Trevin piped in.

Several students laughed. I clenched my fists.

"I wonder if birds are more flammable than humans." Brayce mused. "I suppose we could catch one and try it." He flashed a cruel grin. "What would a bird do if I burned all its feathers off? Would it pretend to be a human like the cur here?"

I took a step toward him. He was too busy laughing at himself to notice. He continued, "It would probably smell better than he does."

The laughter of the students pounded into my ears like a nail being driven by a hammer. I tried to block it out, to control my breathing and keep my heart from racing, but the rage was too strong. It flared at the taunting, and roared to be heard. I blinked, but all I saw was red.

"Maybe it could be his date for the prom," Manny said. Laughter exploded around him.

"And it could pay," Chad said, his deep voice echoing between the buildings.

Everyone paused, trying to make sense of what he said. A few uneasy chuckles sounded when he glanced their way. Brayce grinned at me. "Because a featherless bird would have a better chance at making money than your pathetic excuse of an existence," he explained.

The laughter rolled around me in waves. I couldn't control myself any longer. I was in front of Brayce and had him pinned to the wall faster than Chad could react. The oversized student tried to punch me, but I blocked it with my forearm and slammed the heel of my palm against his chin. He staggered back, his eyes unfocused. The rest of the students stared, too stunned to react.

"You think my existence is pathetic?" I growled, glaring at Brayce as he struggled for air against my tightening grip. "The only reason you pick on the students you do is because they can't fight back. Either they're weaker, afraid, or they'll be expelled. What kind of a coward does that make you?"

Something changed in the air around me. I looked over my shoulder. My heart dropped at the sight of Ava standing on the corner. There was a look of disappointment on her face. I wondered how much she had seen. I dropped Brayce. He fell to the ground gasping for air.

"Ava, I—"

She lifted her beautiful dark gray wings and flew away without waiting for my explanation. I didn't know what she thought of me. If she had appeared only a few seconds before, which is when I felt her watching, all she saw was a Galdoni picking on students.

A roar of frustration tore from my chest. I slammed a fist into the brick wall. Pain ricocheted up my arm. The students backed away, fear in their eyes. Chad pulled Brayce up and practically dragged him down the alley away from me. I hated the fright I saw in everyone's eyes as if they feared I would go after them. Maybe I was as dangerous as they thought.

Filled with disgust at my actions, I walked to the mouth of the alley. Even the sun bathing my wings in golden light wasn't enough to chase away the darkness that filled my thoughts. I flew slowly over the rooftops without the joy that usually filled my flight. If anything, Ava's appearance had made me feel more alone. The look of distress on her face when I had Brayce pinned against the wall was enough to make me believe I truly was an animal. Perhaps I deserved to be expelled.

***

Security had been greatly increased since the new Galdoni Center was built. I landed on the ninth floor and placed my hand on the print reading device near the door. The light turned green and a click sounded to indicate that the door was open.

I crossed the hall to room nine twenty one. It was the closest thing to a home I had ever had; still, I avoided the room whenever possible. The walls were bare and it was free of furnishings besides the bed and a small table for homework. I could have decorated it, but that wasn't my thing. Featureless, it looked a lot like my cell had at the Academy. Needless to say, even my home wasn't my favorite place in the world.

I found Saro assisting on the medical level with his girlfriend Skylar. I waited impatiently for them to finish carrying trays of food to the few residences in the rooms. Saro saw me at the end of the hall and nodded. He said something to Skylar. She smiled and waved at me, then took the tray Saro was carrying and entered one of the rooms. Saro slowed at my look.

"You didn't think it was a good idea to inform me that a girl Galdoni would be showing up at school today?" I demanded when he reached me.

A slight smile lifted his lips. "I thought it would be a nice surprise."

"It wasn't," I informed him flatly.

His smile disappeared. "Reece, what happened?"

I blew out a breath of disgust. "I lost control, that's what happened. And she saw it, which makes it that much worse."

Saro's gaze grew troubled. "Do I need to call Principal Kelley?"

I shook my head. "Not yet. Let's see if Brayce has the guts to tell anyone he and Chad were threatened by *the* Galdoni."

"*The* Galdoni?" he repeated.

I nodded. The remembered frustration burned in my chest; it felt more like humiliation than anything. "That's what they call me there, when they aren't calling me cur," I said quietly.

Saro leaned against the wall. His golden wings hung to either side looking much more regal than my blue wings ever could. Being the only blue-winged Galdoni at the Academy hadn't bothered me. I was tough enough to make questions stop when they started; yet at school, they felt so conspicuous. The fact that the Galdoni integration laws prevented me from hiding them made it worse. No one could fail to notice that I was a Galdoni. I used to think that was good; now I wasn't so sure.

"I can't pretend to know how you feel when it comes to high school," Saro admitted. "I'm still in the social mindset of if it bothers you, hit it. I don't think that works there."

I appreciated his honesty. It didn't help the sting of being ostracized, but the fact that he didn't go immediately to Kale helped. Saro was two years older than me, but sometimes the things I saw in his eyes when he thought no one was looking made him seem so much older.

The skin on the palms of his hands was scarred by burns. I had never asked him what happened; a Galdoni's scars were his own. Yet I still wondered what he had gone through to make him and Kale so close. Whenever I tried to imagine what it would be like to have a family, they were what I pictured, Kale with Brie and Saro with Skylar, one close-knit family who protected each other's backs. That was one family anyone would have to have a death wish to mess with.

"I need to train."

Saro immediately shook his head. "We can't. If anyone finds out that you've broken the integration rules, you'll be out without a chance to go back."

I couldn't meet his gaze. "I know. It's stupid."

He set a hand on my shoulder. "It's not stupid. Fighting is in your blood. I know what it's like to need to hit something so badly you feel like you're going insane. But with this being the first year Galdoni are accepted in schools, we're walking on eggshells. I need to ask you to be patient. Can you do that?"

I nodded. I couldn't do anything else. Saro had watched over me since the Center was rebuilt. Our rooms were next to each other. He was the one who had given me the courage to go to school in the first place. I couldn't let him down; at least not with him knowing it.

"I think I'll grab some dinner," I told him.

"I'm helping Skylar finish up dining services, then we'll be up," he replied, smiling down the hall at Skylar as she pushed a cart laden with trays toward us.

"See you there," I said, trying to sound sincere.

Luckily, his attention was on his girlfriend. It was amazing to see how smitten he was with her, and it also went the other way around. Every time they saw each other, their faces lit up and Saro smiled like he never did with anyone else. He was so different with her, calmer, nicer, as if she brought out the best in him. I wondered how one person could bring out so much in another.

I slipped through the door to the balcony. The new Galdoni Center had been built south of the one that had burned. I could see the small park with the silver statues that marked the memorial to those who had died during the attack. Goliath, the biggest Galdoni at the Center and the

Academy as far as I was aware, had found me in the wreckage of the sixth floor. I had been sleeping like many of the others when the world collapsed around us. If it wasn't for the giant Galdoni, the statues would be a memorial to me as well.

I flew to the tenth floor. The new training facilities were bigger than the last had been, with more fighting rings and better equipped private training rooms. Goliath stood in one corner surveying his small kingdom with his arms crossed and his tan wings hanging loose. Nobody in their right mind would mess with the Galdoni. Occasionally, he took on three or four in a friendly bout that usually ended in sprains and bruises for everyone but him; he kept those events few and far between for all the Galdoni's sake.

I snaked a punch at his ribs. Without looking at me, he caught my fist in his beefy hand and answered it with an open-handed slap to my chest that knocked the wind from me.

"Nice try, Reece."

"Aren't brawny beasts supposed to be the slow ones?" I asked.

He gave a single deep chuckle. "You're confusing me with a human."

I laughed. "Maybe so."

He grinned at me, his wide smile belying his huge size and ability to crush anyone like an ant. "How's school?"

I shook my head. "Not a good subject."

His bushy eyebrows rose. "Girl problems?"

I grimaced. "How is it everyone knew about the girl Galdoni but me?"

He shrugged. "I make it my business to know."

I nodded and repeated the statement he had said many times, "And nobody messes with your business."

He laughed, a deep, rumbly sound. "You got it."

I nodded. "Somebody's messing with my business, Goliath. I need to train."

He frowned and glanced toward the Galdoni training throughout the room. I had already ensured that the closest Galdoni were too busy with staff sequences to overhear us. Goliath must have figured it wasn't worth the risk because he motioned for me to go to his office. I took a seat on the uncomfortable wooden chair he kept near the desk. He had told me once that he had picked the worst chair at the Galdoni Center for any who chose to enter his office; it made them that much more eager to leave. I shifted uncomfortably.

Goliath shut the door. "Per the rules, you're not supposed to train."

I gave him a dry look. "Have you ever known a Galdoni who didn't train?"

He shook his head and took a seat behind the desk. His chair was bigger than some of the couches at the Center, and he loomed over the tiny computer that sat in one corner and was being used as a paperweight. "I thought it was crazy when they passed it, but a rule's a rule."

I stared at the ceiling, hoping for inspiration. "There's also a rule that if I fight, I get expelled for life, but there's no such rule for the students."

I saw his curious look out of the corner of my eye. "Somebody's trying to fight you?"

I nodded and met his gaze. "A student named Brayce and a few of his cronies. He figures if he can get me to punch him, he can get me expelled."

"So he risks being beaten to a pulp by a Galdoni so that he can get rid of you?" Goliath shook his head incredulously. "That's messed up."

I sighed. "Tell me about it. That's why I need to train. I can feel my muscle memory lagging. I need to be able to defend myself without killing him. All I want to do is knock his head off. Maybe if it hurts him enough to attack me and he has nothing to show for it, he'll leave me alone."

Goliath nodded. "Makes sense."

My heart rose, then his expression became troubled. I was worried he would remember the rules.

"You'll have to train in secret."

I nodded, relieved. "I can do that."

He studied me. "I'm sure you can. Meet me in training room G in five minutes."

I thanked him and walked to the balcony. Because of the new print reading system, it would have been faster to use the stairs to go just one floor down, but I used any excuse to fly. I took an extra loop around the building just for kicks before I landed on the ninth floor. I hurried to my room and grabbed my training pants. They were loose and tied at the waist like the pants we had worn at the Academy, but these were made of cotton instead of the scratchy material we had become used to. It was one more reminder of what life had been, and the life Kale had worked to provide for us.

"Going somewhere?"

I turned at Saro's inquisitive look. "I, uh, well," I stammered, wondering how to explain the pants. "I ran into Goliath and he mentioned they needed more clothes on the training level because a few of the Galdoni had ripped theirs. I told him he could use mine because I wasn't allowed to train."

The excuse sounded pretty dumb to me, but Saro nodded. "That's nice of you. Tell him I'll mention the shortage to Kale and have some more ordered."

"I will," I replied in relief.

He turned to leave, then hesitated at the door. "I should have told you about Ava. I understand how a head's up would have been nice."

That brought a smile to my face. "No problem. I don't think anything would have happened differently, but I wouldn't have been caught staring with my mouth open like the rest of the class."

Saro chuckled. "I'll keep that in mind next time."

"Thanks."

I jogged to the balcony with the white training pants held under one arm. It wouldn't do to have anyone else question me. I jumped into the air, pushed my wings down hard, and rose to the tenth floor. The print reader beeped and I hurried inside. Goliath was already waiting near the training room door.

He put a hand on the wall, blocking my path. "Just to be clear, your educational opportunities and my employment are hanging on the fact that you can keep this training a secret."

I nodded. "Trust me; I know."

He studied me a minute longer, than let me pass. I opened the door and was surprised to see a Galdoni with red hair and pale orange wings punching a dummy in the corner. He turned when we entered, and I recognized him as Lem. He was a good friend of Saro's; they often went on missions from Kale together.

"What's going on?" I asked Goliath.

He shrugged. "I asked Lem to train you. I've got a job to do and if I'm missing, people are going to start asking questions."

Lem held out a hand, his green eyes bright. "It'll be nice working together," he said.

I shook his hand. He yanked me forward into a headlock. I grabbed his wrist and drew it over my head, drove a left punch in to his kidney, then dropped and spun, using my leg to sweep his legs out from under him. Anticipating my move, the Galdoni jumped. He landed with his fists ready and a smile on his face.

"Well done. Looks like we're going to have fun together." He rubbed his side where my fist had connected. "Except if you don't want to leave bruises, you're going to have to ignore the impulse to punch your attacker."

"My bad," I replied. My heart was racing. It felt good to give into the impulse to fight. The adrenaline filled me with heat.

"Again?" Lem asked.

I nodded with a grin.

"I'll leave you two to train," Goliath said. "Straighten up when you're done."

Chapter Four

It was well after midnight when I flew back down to the ninth floor. My knuckles throbbed and I would definitely have a few bruises even though we had worn sparring gear. It felt great, like I was doing what I was supposed to, even though I wasn't. I loved the simplicity of fighting. Fists and feet made sense to me. When my body fell into the cadence of combat, it felt like a graceful, deadly dance. I knew where each fall of my foot should be, how each punch should land to create the maximum impact, and where I needed to be afterwards to defend myself. I wished the social aspects of life were as simple.

I paused on the balcony, my hand raised above the print reader. A sound repeated from the floor below. It was muffled, but carried through one of the windows. The eighth floor had been assigned to the female Galdoni Saro and Kale had freed. I seldom saw them because they preferred to keep to themselves. Ava was the first I had actually seen up close. One of them was crying. Something told me I knew who it would be.

I let out a slow breath. I couldn't land on the eighth floor because the print reader wouldn't open. I would have to take the stairs or the elevator. The thought of riding in the little white box made me shudder. I opened the door to the ninth floor balcony and went inside. The downfall of taking the stairs was the cameras. After the last building was attacked, security at the Galdoni Center had become extremely tight. If I went to the eighth floor, I would probably be tracked and stopped.

I crossed the hallway to the door, took a steeling breath, and opened it. A glance at the little dome camera in the corner confirmed my fears. I paused with a hand on the doorknob as memories flooded my thoughts.

I saw a similar camera in a corner covered by a sheet of protective glass. The room was small and grey, the door made of metal and sealed so that only a tiny ray of light showed through when the lights in the hallway were on. I could open the slot in the door that food came through, but it barely made a difference in the darkness. Cold permeated everything. I had to will myself not to shake, because once I started, it was hard to stop. Instead, I kept warm by jogging in place and throwing punches at the ghosts that haunted my mind.

I shook my head to clear the memory. I reminded myself that the camera on the wall was to protect us, not control our actions. I hurried down the stairs.

I pushed open the door to the eighth floor, then hesitated. It was different from the ninth floor. The walls were the same beige color and the speckled marble floor contained matching swirls. Similar comfortable tan couches held residence at each end for those who wanted to sit and talk beneath the wide windows that now bathed the hallway in starlight. It took me a moment to realize what that difference was. I bit back a laugh. It didn't smell like the locker room at Crosby High. Instead, subtle hints of softer scents like flowers and mangos touched the air. Apparently girls smelled better than boys. I wondered if I could get a room transfer.

A muffled sob made my heart twist. I walked down the hall, my sneakers making soft snicks along the floor. I paused by room eight twenty one. Her room was directly below mine. Another sob sounded. It was faint as if she had her face in a pillow. The door was open a crack. I pushed it open slowly.

"Leave me alone."

I froze, my heart hammering in my throat.

"Don't," she protested, her voice tight. "Please don't."

I pushed the door open further. Moonlight spilled across the room from a wide window whose curtains had been thrown aside. My heart slowed at the sight of Ava huddled in a corner of the bed. Her blankets were twisted around her as though she had been struggling all night. Tears streaked her cheeks. Her eyes were closed. She shook her head from side to side.

"Leave me alone. You don't have to do this." The terror in her voice tore through my restraint.

I crossed to her bed and put a hand on her shoulder. "Ava," I whispered.

A small shriek tore from her. She huddled against the wall, her eyes still closed and fear stark on her face. She was still asleep, caught in a tormented dream or memory. I had gone through plenty of those when I left the Academy. I did what Kale had done for me. I wrapped her in my arms.

"Ava, Ava, it's me, Reece." She struggled. Cries of fear filled the room. She tried to get away, clawing at my arms as her wings tried to force free.

"Ava!" I said as loud as I dared without bring security down on us. "Ava, you're alright! Wake up! You're safe, Ava. Listen to me."

Her struggles slowed, then stopped. She was shaking in my arms. For a moment, she froze as if she realized what was going on, then she turned in my arms and put her head against my chest. Her whole body trembled, and I quickly realized I still hadn't put on a shirt from training. Her tears pattered onto my chest. A shiver ran down my spine at the hot and cold that played across my skin.

"You're alright," I whispered into her mussed long black hair.

She shook, the top of her head brushing against my chin. "He was there, and I was tied down. I couldn't get away. He kept. . . ." The words cut off as if she couldn't bring herself to say them. I held her tighter, willing her racing heart to calm as it pounded against my chest.

Anger burned through me at whoever had caused her such terror. I wanted to break every bone in his body, and it still wouldn't be enough suffering for the torment he had caused. "You're safe with me," I said, willing my voice to remain calm. "I'll protect you."

"Thank you," she said. The words came out as a sob.

I leaned against the wall. She huddled closer as if she couldn't feel safe enough. I smoothed the feathers of her wings and used gentle fingertips to brush the tangled hair from the side of her face. It was wet with her tears and refused to obey. I tucked the stray strands behind her ear, wondering at how soft they felt.

I had never held a girl in my arms before. She felt soft and warm even as she continued to shake in my arms. I used my foot to scoot her blanket within reach. When I could grab it, I wrapped it over her wings so that it settled around her shoulders. A small sigh escaped her. Her eyes were closed. She was almost asleep, but the tears continued to trickle down her face.

"You're alright, Ava," I whispered. Night terrors had tormented me for almost two months straight after I left the Academy. Memories of training, classmates dying, and the never-ending crack of whips still brought me to my knees at the most unexpected times. The fact that whatever had been done to Ava was enough to cause the same terror meant it was something truly horrible. All I could do was hold her.

Her breathing eventually steadied and the tears stopped falling. Her hands loosened their grip around me, and her body stopped trembling. Still, I sat there. I couldn't find it in myself to leave her on her bed, alone and scared if the terrors came back.

There was something else. Being with her, holding her, made me feel different. It was as if I was strong enough to help someone, instead of *the* Galdoni who messed everything up and was a target. I had done something good. Now wasn't the time to blow it.

Eventually, I eased her head carefully onto the pillow. Her breath caught, then resumed again. The smallest of smiles touched her face. I stood still, captivated that I could even be in the same room with something so beautiful. The smile faded and her eyebrows pulled together.

I wanted to touch her cheek, to soothe the troubled look and let her know she was alright, but such a touch might send her into sobs again. I let out a slow breath and left her room. I shut the door to a small crack like it had been when I entered. I waited for several minutes to ensure she was sleeping soundly, then went back to the stairs.

It took a long time for sleep to steal through my restless mind. I kept waking with the thought that she was crying again. Sounds of her terror played in my head, tormenting my dreams. I wanted to help her, but I wasn't able. I could never find her. She was lost in my dreams.

***

The next morning, I sat at a breakfast table with Kale, Brie, Saro, and Skylar. A few more Galdoni were scattered around the room, but most were either still sleeping or were training with Goliath.

"You went to her room?" Saro asked, surprise clear in his voice.

I shrugged, keeping my attention on my oatmeal. I swirled the fresh strawberries around as I replied, "I couldn't just leave her crying."

I saw Kale nod out of the corner of my eye. "Was she alright?"

"No," I replied. I stared at the table, remembering. "She kept saying things, but she was asleep. She was crying uncontrollably." I looked at Kale. "I did what you did for me."

It was hard to say the words out loud. Galdoni were trained to never show vulnerability. Kale had been there for me at my weakest moments. He had seen me at my worst, and helped me through it. I had been fourteen and a half when the Academy closed. The memories were so stark and real. Now at sixteen, they still had a hard enough grip to make my breath catch in my throat.

"You held her until she could sleep," Kale replied quietly. Brie's arm slipped through his and she gave him a sweet smile that he returned.

I nodded. "It took a while. She had been pretty scared, but it was hard for her to wake up."

"Poor girl," Skylar said. "I can't imagine what she's been through."

"Did you stay there all night?" Saro asked.

"Are you kidding?" I replied. "I was afraid she would wake up and remember that she hated me."

Kale chuckled. "It can't be as bad as that."

Saro was about to answer him when the group grew quiet. Everyone looked past me. I turned and saw that Ava had entered the cafeteria. She met my gaze, her expression curious. After a second, she turned away to join the female Galdoni on the other side of the lunchroom. Alana and Jayce scooted over to make room for her. Even though Jayce was a human, none of the female Galdoni seemed to mind his presence. He and Alana were inseparable. I never saw one without the other.

While I was happy for them, their bliss made my mistakes that much more apparent. I ate the rest of my breakfast in silence, oblivious to the conversations around me. When I rose, Kale stood also. "I'll catch you in a bit," he told Brie. She kissed him and sat back down with Skylar to continue their discussion on the current hot guys in movies.

"What about the guy with the dog?" Saro piped in. "They're pretty good at solving crimes."

"Are you talking about Scooby-Doo?" Skylar asked. At his nod, all three of them burst out laughing.

Kale and I set our trays in the washroom where we all rotated the cleaning duties. He led the way into the hall and walked to the end near the window.

"She begged me to let her go to school," he said quietly.

I shook my head. "I don't think she's ready."

A humorless smile curved his lips. "Are any of us?"

I opened my mouth to argue, then lowered my gaze. "Not really."

He nodded. "She needed some semblance of a normal life. She hoped that if she went to school and got into a regular schedule, it would help her move on from everything that had happened."

"What did happen?" I asked, even though I wasn't sure I wanted to know.

Kale glanced toward the cafeteria. "She should be the one to tell you that."

I nodded. "That's fair."

He put a hand on my shoulder. "I appreciate you being there for her last night. Please watch out for her at school. You know it's not easy being different."

"I think she already has friends," I told him, a bit bothered that I hadn't made the same progress. Seth was the only one who even cared if I showed up.

"I'm glad to hear it," Kale replied. "I'm sure that will help." His phone buzzed. He glanced at the message. "I've got to go. Have a good day at school."

"Thanks."

I watched him hurry up the hall. I had school in a half hour, but something made me follow him. He left through the balcony and landed on the sixth floor, the children's block. I followed as close behind as I dared. When the print reader beeped and the door opened, chaos erupted.

Children were running and screaming. Several were crying. I spotted Saro's girlfriend Skylar in one corner holding two toddlers whose wings were still covered in fuzzy down. Her face was white and her blue eyes were tight with worry. In the other corner, the source of the madness became clear.

Two Galdoni children were fighting. One had curly blond hair and dark red wings, the other had gray wings held tight against his back as he wielded a knife. Both couldn't have been more than twelve, but they held the weapons as if they were ready to use them, the benefits of an Academy upbringing.

Kale was already behind the gray-winged Galdoni; neither had noticed him, their attention focused solely on each other. That was where the youthfulness of their training was evident. By the time Galdoni were old enough to begin Arena training, they knew to watch for external threats as well as those that were obvious. Yet it put Kale in a bad position. If he tried to take the knife from the young Galdoni, he would be open to attack from the second. It wouldn't be a problem if he could just take them out, but they were children and he no doubt wanted them unscathed.

I circled close to the wall and positioned myself behind the red-winged Galdoni's back. Kale nodded at me. He mouthed one, two, three. We both sprang forward and wrapped our arms around the fighting boys. I trapped the Galdoni's red wings against his back and caught his wrist while I pinned down the other arm. A quick glance showed that he only had a small paring knife as a weapon. At his feet I noticed there were white shavings.

Near Kale's foot as he struggled to calm the other boy down was a creature carved from a block of what looked like soap. It had apparently been a dragon, but someone had cut off the head and wings; I realized it was the source of the fight.

The Galdoni boy I held didn't struggle. I would normally have been prepared for an elbow to the stomach and a sweep with the legs as we had been taught, but he merely stood there in acceptance that the fight was over. Kale, on the other hand, had been forced to pin the other Galdoni on the ground in order to remove the knife and keep him from throwing punches.

"What happened?" Kale asked.

Skylar had calmed the other children enough to explain. "Ransom pulled the knife from somewhere and destroyed

Koden's dragon. He's been working on that for a week. Kara just left and Sarel should be here, but I couldn't separate them and protect the children."

Kale nodded. "You did great, Skylar. You kept the children safe." He looked down at the Galdoni. "Can I let you up?"

Ransom gave a noncommittal grunt.

Kale rose warily, positioning himself between Ransom and Koden who stood next to me without a word. The red-winged boy merely watched his aggressor. His stance wasn't ready for defense, and from what I could tell, he appeared completely calm considering the fact that he had just been attacked with a knife. Sometimes I wished our training at the Academy hadn't been quite so thorough. I wondered if the children Galdoni would ever be ready for school.

"Why did you destroy Koden's dragon?" Kale asked Ransom.

Ransom shrugged. "I wanted it, and he wouldn't give it to me." His eyes were on the knife in Kale's hand.

Kale's gaze shifted to it. "Where did you get this?"

"The training room," Ransom said quietly without meeting Kale's gaze.

Kale's brow furrowed. "Real weapons are locked up. Only Goliath has the key."

Ransom shrugged again. "I'm good with locks."

Kale blew out a slow breath. He glanced at Skylar. "That seems to be a trend."

She gave a slight smile, pushing her short black and red hair from her face. "Perhaps we need better locks."

Kale nodded. "I'll take care of it." He turned his attention back to the boy. "Ransom, you know it's not right to attack someone just because you want what he has."

"At the Academy, I was taught to take what I wanted. It was mine if I won." There was defiance in Ransom's voice, but also confusion.

Kale glanced at me. My heart went out to him. Life outside the Academy was new for all of us. Even though it had been closed for almost two years, I still battled my training every day. Kale tipped the boy's head up with gentle fingers. I was surprised to see tears in the boy's green eyes.

Kale's expression filled with pity. "What we learned at the Academy was right for there, but we aren't in the Academy anymore."

"I don't understand," Ransom replied. He closed his eyes, refusing to let the tears fall. "I know how to fight."

Kale crouched down so that they were eye level. The boy opened his eyes again. "Sometimes knowing when not to fight can be even more powerful."

Kale looked at Koden. "Are you alright?"

Koden nodded. He glanced up at me as if to ascertain whether I felt otherwise. I gave him a smile I hoped was confident. He walked to Kale and stooped to pick up the destroyed dragon. Sadness showed on his face at the damage that had been done, but he didn't say anything. He wandered toward Skylar's side of the classroom, his attention on the soap carving. As soon as he was clear of us, children ran to meet him, following him quietly to a corner where he sat and began working again.

I looked back at Kale. He was talking quietly to Ransom. "Our instincts are to fight; that's the answer we were given. Here, though, we have many other answers, including speaking to someone when we want something."

"Koden doesn't talk," Ransom replied as though frustrated about it. "He's a freak."

Kale glanced over his shoulder. I followed his gaze to Koden who watched us silently. None of the other children appeared to have heard, but it was obvious by the hurt in the boy's eyes that he had. At our attention, he focused back on his soap.

Kale set a hand on Ransom's shoulder. The boy shrugged it off. "He didn't answer when I asked him if I could have the dragon. Ignoring someone is stupid; it says he doesn't think I'm a threat. I had to prove I was a threat."

I could hear the Academy training in his words. It pained me to see Ransom's confusion. The steps he followed were straight from the teachings for his age group that were drilled into the students until they practiced the rules as easily as breathing. To have life and all the rules change as stark as night and day didn't seem fair to me, either.

"You did what you felt you needed to," Kale continued. "Your response is understandable. I just want to teach you to think through your actions so that you are acting with thought instead of instinct."

"When thought, instinct, and action are one, the warrior's journey is complete," Ransom recited.

Kale's eyes closed briefly. I felt his pain. I had heard the same sentence recited by hundreds of mouths. He let out a slow breath and opened his eyes again. "Ransom, I created this place so that Galdoni can be free to think their own thoughts. You don't have to be a warrior anymore."

Ransom's eyebrows pulled together. "What else is there?"

Kale smiled. "I'll show you."

"Promise?" Ransom asked.

Kale's smile deepened. "I promise. There is more to life than fighting. You just have to decide what you want to do."

"What I want to do," Ransom repeated quietly as though the statement tasted strange in his mouth.

Kale stood. "Just promise me you won't get any more weapons from Goliath's vault."

Ransom nodded. "I promise."

Kale glanced at me. "Thanks, Reece. I think we've got it from here. You have school to get to, don't you?"

My heart dropped. I glanced at the clock in the corner. I had five minutes before the bell rang. "Gotta go!" I told him and Skylar.

"Thanks, Reece," Skylar called after me as I ran for the balcony.

I lifted a hand in reply, pulled open the door, and jumped over the edge.

Chapter Five

"The principal called you to his office," Seth said the instant I set foot inside the school. He ran up wheezing as though he had run all over the school looking for me. "I couldn't find you. He's been paging you over the intercom for the last ten minutes."

"I had to help Kale with the kids at the Center," I explained, following him slower than he wanted me to as was obvious by the way he hurried toward the office and then jogged back for me to follow.

"Kale!" he replied. Seth was in awe of the Galdoni who had shut down the Arena. To me, Kale was an amazing guy, but to Seth he was a superstar. It made me smile to hear the awe in his voice.

"Yeah; everything's fine."

"Is it?"

We both looked up at the sound of Principal Kelley's deep voice. Seth let out a little squeak and froze. The last bell rang; we were both late for class.

"It's alright," I reassured Seth. "I'll catch you later."

He turned without a word and began running down the hall, his sneakers squeaking on the tile floor.

"No running, Mr. Gibson," Principal Kelley shouted.

Seth stopped so quickly he almost fell over. He righted himself. "S-sorry, Principal Kelley," he called. He continued with measured steps toward his classroom.

Principal Kelley turned without a word and walked through the front office.

"Good morning, Reece," Mrs. Jeffrey said. Her voice was uncertain as though she wondered if seeing me really indicated that it was a good morning.

"Good morning, Mrs. Jeffrey," I replied.

She turned her attention back to the paperwork on her desk as though she couldn't get to it fast enough.

I followed Principal Kelley to the office on the right. He took a seat behind the wide brown desk. I sat in the center chair of three metal ones pulled up to the other side of his desk. The chair was ice cold. I wondered if he had a way to chill them before students came to his office as one more way to signify their impending doom.

Principal Kelley leaned his elbows on the black mat on his desk and linked his fingers together. He gave me a stern look over them.

"Reece, I would like nothing better than to dismiss you for brawling with Brayce Bryant."

"I didn't take him for the snitching type," I replied.

The principal's eyes narrowed. "His mother called to complain about the bruises on her son's neck. Apparently you're not so good at hiding the signs of your aggression."

"I'll get better at that," I muttered.

Principal Kelley's teeth ground so loud I could hear them in the silence. He let out a slow breath, his eyes pinning me and his toupee skewed slightly on his head. "As I said, I would like nothing better than to kick you out of my school."

I nodded, accepting the inevitable. "Alright."

He shook his head, surprising me. "Unfortunately, the government gave us a hefty funds increase as the result of taking in a *Galdoni*," he spat the word, "as one of our students. With only ten other schools in the state willing to do so, and one Galdoni male allowed per school, they are very pleased with our cooperation and have continued to show their gratitude financially. Now with Ava added, that appreciation has doubled." He sighed. "I've already signed the contract on the new basketball court and they've began construction on the swimming pool for the swim team."

He rubbed his eyes beneath glasses with transition lenses that adjusted to the light. In the neon glare from his humming light overhead, I could see the aversion in his gaze at having a Galdoni in his office. "Currently, it is almost impossible to get a job without a high school diploma even for the best qualified. If you quit, it'll be most assuredly impossibly for you being that you're a, well, what you are. If I kick you out, per the integration laws you will no longer be allowed in any school, anywhere. So it is in your best interest to stay at Crosby High." He let out a sigh of defeat. "Apparently we're stuck with each other."

"Do all of your students receive such a welcome?" I asked.

He grimaced. "Only those with feathers."

I wanted to punch him. I didn't care about myself. I didn't matter in the grand schemes of Crosby High; but I cared about the kids at the Galdoni Center who might one day follow in my footsteps. If they met such a greeting at school, perhaps it would be better off if they didn't go. But if what Principal Kelley said about jobs was true? What would the Galdoni do when they got older?

I left the room without replying to the principal's statement. When I passed Mrs. Jeffrey's desk, her head was bent and her gaze was studiously averted from mine. I let out a sigh of frustration and left the office.

When I reached algebra, I remembered that Ava would be there. I was almost ready to smile when I entered the classroom. The students looked up as they always did when someone opened the door. Mr. Bennett gave a brief nod that said Mrs. Jeffrey had notified him over the speaker of my late arrival; so she had indeed noticed my departure. I nodded back and turned my attention to Ava.

She was also pointedly not looking in my direction. I paused by her desk, but she continued talking to the brunette in the next seat. I crossed to my seat in the back of the classroom and threw my algebra book on the desk hard enough that everyone jumped. I slumped and stared out the window. School hadn't been my favorite place before the day started, and it was quickly going downhill from there.

***

I waited at the door to the lunchroom for Ava to appear. The second she and her friends turned the corner, I approached her. "What gives, Ava?" I demanded, too tired of the events of the day to care about my tone.

She looked at her friends who watched us with wide eyes as though worried I was about to kill her. "Excuse us," she said politely.

She grabbed the sleeve of my shirt and proceeded to tow me into the hallway. I would have fought back, but the action surprised me so much I could only follow.

"Seriously?" she said the second we were out of earshot. She shoved me against the wall. "You're demanding what's up with me?"

I put up my hands. "I'm sorry about what you saw the other day with Brayce's gang. You don't know half of the story."

"Don't I?" Ava shot back. "From what I hear, everyone is afraid of you. You don't smile, you don't have friends, and you look like you're ready to tear someone apart if they so much as look at you wrong. Galdoni are killers; I guess I was hoping to hear you were different."

I stared at her. Her words tore my heart out and stomped on it. I could barely breathe. I felt deflated, empty. I didn't know what I had been expecting, but it definitely wasn't this. I struggled to find my thoughts. What came out was only darkness. "I didn't choose my origin," I said, my tone flat to hide the heartache in my voice. "I was trained to be a killer, and I didn't choose that, either." I gritted my teeth to keep my emotions hidden. "I didn't ask to slice flesh with swords and knives and watch other Galdoni bleed. I didn't ask to hit bags and dummies until my knuckles split and fingers refused to work. I didn't ask to be beaten and thrown in cells so dark time didn't matter because it all blurred into the same meaningless existence."

If there was surprise or compassion on her face, I didn't see it. Instead, I saw blood on my fingers again. It was my blood, trailing down my arm from a knife wound MF270 had put there. I watched him be praised for the cut. We were seven. I couldn't understand why my pain meant someone else's reward. The world didn't make sense.

I shook my head to clear the memory and looked at Ava. She took a step back as if shocked by what she saw. "You cannot choose your origin, Ava. You can only choose what you make of it."

I was done. I couldn't stand being inside the school one more minute. The walls felt like they were closing in. The bricks leered at me, laughing at the fact that a Galdoni pretended to be a student. I couldn't breathe.

I shoved past Ava and ran for the door. I heard her call my name. I pushed the front doors open, one and then the other. Fresh air rushed against me. I fell to my knees on the sidewalk, gulping in huge breaths. Tears fell down my cheeks. I couldn't control my thoughts. I couldn't force the memories away. I was chained against a wall and beaten, the rattle of the chains loud in my ears. I was kneeling on cold cement breathing in warm air. I was lying in a puddle of blood, cringing against the laughter of the enforcer who had beaten me at six years old for taking an extra piece of bread.

"Reece?" Ava said softly.

I rose and spun; she backed off, her hands raised as if afraid I would hit her.

The look destroyed what remained of my will. "You don't know me, Ava," I said in defeat. "How dare you judge me when you have no idea what I've been through?" I gestured weakly toward the school. "You're just like the rest of them."

I raised my wings. I didn't care if I was on school property. After our little talk, I realized Principal Kelley cared more about money for his school than one student he felt was beneath him. I was so tired of being beneath everyone. I flew into the sky.

Ava called my name again. I ignored her and flew faster. I dodged between buildings and forced my wings down harder. A faint cloud cover trailed over the sky, filtering the sunlight so that it reached below with only half of its strength. I broke through the clouds. Warmth bathed my face, drying my tears. I took in a huge breath and held it as I pushed my wings slowly to keep me in one place.

"I've never flown like that!"

Ava's voice broke through the calm I had found. I let out the breath slowly and glanced at her. "You should be at the school."

"You should, too," she replied. "I'm so sorry, Reece."

The warmth and regret in her apology ate at my heart. "You don't have to be," I said, turning my face back toward the sun so she wouldn't see how her words affected me.

She touched my arm. "I am," she said. "I shouldn't have listened to them. You deserve more than that."

"I don't deserve anything," I replied softly without looking at her.

"Everyone deserves a chance," she said.

It was her tone that made me look back. Her eyes were lowered. Sunlight played along her black hair, bringing out red and gold highlights amid the darkness. It bathed her cheeks and gray wings so that she looked like an angel, an angel who had broken my heart.

CHEREE ALSOP

Yet I didn't feel pain when I looked at her, because her last statement hadn't been for me. I saw it in the line of her mouth and the way her eyebrows drew together. There were tears in her green eyes that she refused to let fall.

"Everyone deserves a chance?" I repeated her statement gently as a question.

"Maybe not," she said, meeting my gaze. The depth to her eyes almost made me forget to fly. There was so much heartache and pain, loss and betrayal that I wondered how I had ever been jealous at her easy entrance into Crosby High. If anyone needed a friend, it was her.

"Ava, what happened to you?" I asked quietly.

She shook her head. "I can't talk about it. Not yet."

I nodded. "You don't have to."

She let out a breath and turned her face toward the sun. "I feel so much stronger up here," she said with her eyes closed. "Like the sun gives me strength." A smile touched the corners of her mouth. "Like Superman."

"Who?" I asked.

Her eyes opened and she looked at me. "Don't tell me you don't know who Superman is."

I shook my head. "Kind of a pretentious name, isn't it?"

She laughed, a wonderful sound that made my heart give a little skip as though it was delighted. I was sure that couldn't have been good for me. I put a hand to my chest. "You should probably get back. They might miss you."

She looked down at the buildings below, then glanced back up at me. Her eyelashes hid her gaze as if she was suddenly shy. "They might miss you, too."

I shook my head, but it was with more amusement than pain that I replied, "Nobody misses me. I'll go back eventually."

"Promise?" she asked.

I nodded and she smiled at me. "I hope so, Reece."

She tucked her wings and I watched her dive gracefully through the clouds. When she disappeared from view, I turned my face back toward the sun feeling just a bit better.

Chapter Six

That night I took my food up to the empty study hall. I felt so pent up that I couldn't face the other Galdoni, even to eat. The silence pressed in around me, threatening to drive me mad. The elevator opened. I glanced up, then bowed my head again when Saro saw me hunched in the corner, my food forgotten on the table.

He sat down against the wall without a word. I avoided his gaze. Instead, I traced a faint scar across my knuckles a Galdoni's teeth had left there at the Academy. I remembered the blood from my hand and his mouth. When it mixed together, it looked the same. I couldn't understand what there was to fight about.

"Scars leave more damage on the heart than the skin," Saro said quietly.

I glanced at him. He frowned, his attention on the window by my side. The darkness left little to be seen but his reflection.

"Sometimes I feel like I don't have enough scars for the way I feel," I replied in a voice barely above a whisper.

I saw Saro nod out of the corner of my eye. "At the Academy, it was the scars that defined us. It took me a long time to get past that."

"Now what defines you?" I asked.

A slight smile touched his lips. He let out a small sigh. "I suppose it's my stubbornness. Skylar says she's grateful I'm so stubborn because I wouldn't be here without it."

"She's glad you're stubborn?" I repeated; a reluctant smile touched my lips at the thought.

Saro pulled up his shirt. My stomach twisted at the sight of a long, thick, ugly scar that worked its way from near his bellybutton to his back. His chest was covered in scars that made a thick patchwork of raised skin. There was a big round circle by his shoulder and another through his stomach that looked as though he had been stabbed by something.

I didn't know what to say. Saro pulled his shirt back down as if he guessed as much. "Not a pretty sight, but I'm alive."

"Did you get all those in the Arena?"

He shook his head. "Surprisingly enough, I got the majority of them afterwards."

I tipped my head against the wall. "Sometimes I wish I had been old enough to fight in the Arena."

Saro was silent for a few minutes. When he finally spoke, his voice was quiet. "I wouldn't wish that on anyone. Death should never be taken so lightly."

I let out a breath. "I don't want to kill anyone. It's just. . . ." I searched for the right words. I held up my hands. "I just feel like there's something inside of me waiting to explode. I'm worried if I keep getting pushed, I'm not going to be able to control it and someone will get hurt."

Saro nodded. "Going against our nature isn't easy. There's a reason Kale picked you to be one of the first for the Galdoni integration program."

Surprised, I glanced at him. "What's the reason?"

The gold-winged Galdoni leaned his head against the bricks and smiled. "It was the way you handled yourself at the Academy."

I shook my head. "That was nearly two years ago. I had to fight and I trained like the rest."

"But there was something that linked you, Kale, and me together. You hated hurting people. It was obvious by the way you fought, and you got beaten more because of it." He chuckled. "The three of us definitely spent plenty of time in solitary."

Things began to make sense. "Is that why he chose the other nine Galdoni that are at the other schools?"

Saro nodded. "We needed Galdoni who believed we can be more than we were told we could be. Fighting against hurting others at the Academy went against self-preservation and instinct. Those who were brave enough to do so were punished accordingly." A slight smile touched his face. "It's funny how punishment can sometimes feel better than giving others pain."

I understood the sentiment exactly. "I knew if I was being punished, someone else was being saved the same."

Saro glanced at me. "Kale chose wisely."

"I don't know about that." I looked at my hands. "What if I can't do it? What if I can't control myself?"

He turned his attention back to the window. "We all have regrets. We each have our own trials and tests that set us apart because we're individuals. Even though we were created in test tubes, we aren't clones; we have our own drives and ambitions." He smiled, but his eyes shone with what I realized were tears. "I have many regrets, Reece. My goal now is to live so that I don't create any more."

"You're doing a better job than I am," I admitted.

He glanced at me. "What makes you say that?"

I let the words spill out. "I'm afraid to live, Saro. I'm worried that if I let down my guard for even a second, I'll mess up and everything you and Kale have been trying to accomplish will be destroyed. I'm afraid he chose wrong, that I can't handle it." I dropped my face into my hands. "I'm afraid of the part of me that wants to fight and longs to kill."

Saro was silent for a minute. When he spoke again, his voice was soft. "When they made the Galdoni, they did so with the hope of creating the perfect soldier. But they messed up. We were too aggressive, but also too independent. They wanted soldiers who could fly with bombs and be undetectable by radar, but they also wanted warriors who would obey their commands without question. They messed up when they gave us human DNA. We had minds of our own and rebelled against control."

I watched him, surprised at the details of our origin I didn't know.

"The government had put so much tax money into the experiments that they couldn't admit they had made a mistake. Instead, they figured out a way to make that money back."

"Taxes from gambling on the fights," I said.

He nodded. "And it worked. They made so much more than they ever put in." He rubbed the back of his neck. "Now, thanks to Kale, we're free with the expectations of settling into society. It's easy for everyone to assume we can shove our violent nature to the background, but it was a part of us the moment we were created."

"So what do we do?" I asked.

He smiled. "Hone it. Make it work for you instead of against you. Take the aggression and put it into your drive to succeed. Show them that you're more than the animal they expect you to be. You already proved that at the Academy. It's easier now without whips ready to say otherwise. Go against the violent side of your Galdoni nature and create your own life."

"I'll try," I said.

"I believe in you," Saro replied, rising to his feet. He smiled down at me. "You can do anything, Reece. Believe in yourself as much as Kale and I believe in you, and you'll be unstoppable."

***

"Good; now break right and follow it with an elbow," Lem instructed.

I did as he said, rolling from his grip on the ground and driving an elbow up at his face.

He blocked the blow and laughed. "If you break your opponent's nose, someone's gonna notice. I thought the point was to leave no evidence."

I nodded. "Then how would you do it?"

He gestured for me to trade him places. With the same roll, he brought up his elbow, but instead of using it against my face, he brought it against the side of my neck while at the same time bringing his other hand to force the elbow that was holding up my weight to bend. The result slammed me against the ground and left me vulnerable to his follow-up. He had my pinned in seconds.

I chuckled with my face against the mat. "Who cleans these things?"

He laughed and stepped back to allow me to rise. "That's how I would do it."

I rubbed my neck. "A bit archaic, don't you think?"

His eyebrows rose. "How would you do it?"

I gestured for him to take his place again, and dropped onto my hands and knees on the practice floor. I let him grab my right wrist and pull it behind me as we had started. The motion bent my wing, but I used the pain to focus my actions.

I grabbed his left hand and rammed my shoulder against him, throwing both our weights into it. He fell to his back and I rolled across him to a crouched position. I landed two soft taps with my fist on his chin, then followed it with a two-fisted slam to the chest that would have broken his sternum and ribs given the right amount of force.

He chuckled and pushed up to a sitting position. "How are you planning to explain that to the board?"

I shrugged. "I figured if I got desperate enough to do that, the board wouldn't take the time to speak to me, they would just throw me in jail."

He grinned. "Always the victim."

Anger rose in my chest. I speared him with a look. "Never the victim."

He raised his hands in defense. "Alright, alright; I'm just kidding. You've got to watch that trigger. With you, it's words. You can't take a joke. You've got to learn to let them roll off your shoulders as you would a punch."

I shook my head. "It's not that easy."

Lem's gaze grew serious. "It has to be that easy," he replied. "If you get defensive every time someone says something that bothers you, that's a weakness. Remember your training; some of it still holds true. If you reveal weakness, humans will prey on it as quickly as a Galdoni, except it's a verbal attack instead of a physical one."

As much as I didn't want to admit it, his words made sense.

He lifted an eyebrow. "Shall we practice?"

I let out a sigh at the laughter in his tone. He was going to enjoy it. "Fine."

***

After a full two hours of being called every rude name in the book, I was done training. Lem chuckled and rubbed his ribs where I had let my temper get the best of me; my back ached where he had answered with a punch hard enough to bruise ribs.

"Don't give up, Reece. Everything takes practice," he reminded me as we left the practice room.

"Except I think you're enjoying our practice sessions a little too much," I replied, grimacing.

"Words can be mightier than the sharpest blade," he said.

I waved him off. He merely laughed and went to find Goliath. I was sure both Galdoni would get a kick out of the verbally abusive training regimen Lem had come up with to add to the defensive fighting techniques. Usually, the thought of others laughing at me made me upset; at the moment, I was too tired to care. Perhaps Lem's lessons were starting to sink in.

Chapter Seven

I paused near the stairs. I couldn't hear any sounds. I didn't have a good reason to check on Ava, but I couldn't fight the urge to make sure she was alright. I walked down the stairs and quietly opened the door at the bottom. My shoes sounded loud on the marble as I crossed the silent eighth floor. I paused before I reached Ava's room.

"Is that you, Reece?" There was fear in her voice.

I walked to her door. "Yes, Ava. Sorry if I woke you. I was trying to be quiet, but—" I heard her sniff and pushed the door open further.

She was huddled in the same corner, her blankets askew and her hair mussed as though she had slept restlessly. Her eyes were filled with tears. I hurried to her side. "I wanted to make sure you were okay."

She shook her head. "I'm not okay," she said in a soft voice. I noticed that her hands were trembling as she tried to smooth the blankets around her without much success.

I caught up her hands in mine and slid onto the bed. She immediately scooted closer, leaning against me. She sat up again and glanced at me. I realized I had forgotten to put a shirt on again. My cheeks flushed with embarrassment. "I was training with Lem. We don't wear shirts because we get too hot and sweaty." I paused. "Which I now realize is the same reason I should have pulled on a shirt before I came here."

She smiled in light of my discomfort. "It was nice of you to check on me." Her tears shone in her eyes.

I looked down at her. "I hoped you didn't need to be checked on."

Something filled her gaze, an emotion that grabbed my heart and refused to let go. "You did?"

My thoughts fled as I stared down at her. "I, uh, well, I just wanted you to sleep good and I hoped—"

"That I didn't need you?" she asked quietly.

I shook my head quickly. "No, not that. It's more that I was worried and I thought, well," I let out a sigh of frustration at the betrayal of my brain. "It's good to be needed."

She smiled at that and wiped her tears away with the corner of her blanket. "You're different than when you're at school."

I nodded. "There's a reason for that." I couldn't deny the searching look she gave me. I was starting to realize that I couldn't deny her anything. I closed my eyes and she put her head against my chest.

I spoke with my chin brushing her hair. "My first day of school was on a Wednesday about six months ago. School had only been going for a month by the time the integration laws passed. Kale hoped that since it was so close to the start of the year, I would be able to fit in."

I took a breath and let the memories of that day swarm over me. I had been filled with anticipation and excitement. I had been naïve. "I was jumped in the hallway right after second period. Brayce's gang and a bunch of other students dragged me into the boys' bathroom." I felt Ava's muscles tense. I held her closer. "They beat me with books and bats. I didn't defend myself."

"Why not?" she asked when I fell silent.

I let myself say what I had felt that day, as painful as it was to admit. "I wanted to snap their arms and legs. I wanted to break their skulls against the tiled wall. I wanted to disembowel them and let them bleed to death on the floor. I wanted to be the very killer you accused me of, because that's how I was raised." I shook my head and whispered, "I'll leave if you want me to."

She was quiet for a moment. I was about to rise when she shook her head against my chest. "I've felt all of that and more for the people who hurt me. I don't think you can help it when you're unable to fight." She looked up at me, understanding so bare in her beautiful green eyes I wanted to ask her who had made her feel such hatred so that I could make them pay. "Why didn't you defend yourself?" she asked again gently.

I looked at the wall across from us. Her room had pictures on the walls of sunrises and beautiful scenery. The picture I looked at was of an old barn with the sun showing through its slats. The grass around it was green and bright with warmth. It looked as though you could step into the frame and never look back, content to live in the simplicity of the moment forever.

"I didn't want to let Kale and Saro down," I admitted. "So much was riding on the ten of us who had been deemed able to start school. If I messed things up at Crosby, other Galdoni would pay."

"What happened to the students who beat you?" she asked.

"They got reprimanded."

"And you?" she continued, her voice quiet.

"I got threatened with expulsion if I caused another fight. Principal Kelley called Kale. I could hear them talking on the phone." A slight smile came to my face. "Kale never asked me about it. I think he knew what had happened. But he pulled me aside the next day before I left and said that if I ever found myself backed into a corner, to give as much as I got."

She gave a small laugh at that. It made me smile to hear it. "I sure like Kale," she said.

I nodded. "He's great guy, and Saro, too."

She lay against my chest for a few more minutes, both of us content just to be. Eventually, she pulled away. "I don't think I'll be sleeping tonight. Want to watch Superman?"

She rose and opened a drawer, then held up the movie proudly.

"Where did you get that?" I asked in surprise.

She handed it to me. "Skylar let me borrow it from the Center's library. She gave me a key so we could watch it whenever we wanted."

At my lifted eyebrows, she laughed. "It's good to have friends."

I nodded. "Guess I should make some."

She pushed my shoulder. "Come on."

I followed her to the door, then hesitated in the hallway. "I should probably grab a shirt."

She threw me a smile that brought a blush to her cheeks. "I don't think you need one."

She led the way to the stairs and I followed wordlessly.

***

"Reece, come join us."

I looked around in surprise. Ava was waving from the big round table she shared with five of the cheerleaders. They looked equally surprised that she had called to me.

I carried my tray slowly toward their table, feeling the stares of the others students on me as I did so. I hesitated at the sight of the empty chair Ava had pulled over.

"I, uh, like to be outside," I said.

"He prefers to eat with the birds," one of the girls explained. I looked at her. A blush rushed across her cheeks as if she had just realized how the sentence came out. She opened her mouth with an apologetic look, but Ava saved her the trouble.

"Too much time behind walls," she said with an understanding smile.

I smiled back with a nod.

Ava stood up. "Let's all go eat outside."

Her friends stared at her as if she was crazy.

She turned away without giving them a choice. I glanced back to see the girls exchange looks, then rise and follow us.

It felt surreal to lead Ava and five other girls to the trees that lined the soccer field. As soon as I sat down, birds landed in the tree branches over our heads and started to chirp.

"What are they doing?" Ava asked.

The girls sat down around us and looked up at the birds.

"Waiting for their lunch," I said. I crumbled a piece of bread from the top of my ham sandwich and spread it on the grass next to me. The birds immediately flew down and began to eat.

"That's neat!" Emily, the brunette cheerleader, exclaimed. "Give them some of yours, Sam."

Sam, the girl who had told Ava about the birds in the cafeteria, immediate tore the crust off her bread and threw it to the birds. They flew over and began pecking at it. "They're so cute!" she exclaimed.

"Sparrows," a girl with short blonde hair said. At everyone's surprised looks, she shrugged. "My dad's a birdwatcher. Those are sparrows, the black ones are starlings, and that one with the red breast is a robin."

"Here robin," Alice, the head cheerleader, called, throwing two French fries at the bird. Two starlings swooped in to steal them. "Hey!" she protested.

Feeling a bit brave, I whispered to Ava, "Watch this." I held out a piece of bread.

The little sparrow I had come to recognize from my many trips to the tree hopped toward me. His head was darker than the others and one of his wings hung slightly askew like it had been broken once, though he flew as if it didn't bother him.

"Oh my goodness," Ava exclaimed softly as the bird took the bread from my hand.

I smiled and handed him another piece. He took it and flew away. When I looked back, Ava was watching me as though I was completely different than she had expected. The look sent a rush of warmth through me.

Footsteps heralded Seth's approach. I smiled at the look of shock on his face. "What, I mean, why. . . ."

I tipped my head to indicate a spot on the grass. "Just sit down," I replied.

"Gladly!" He took a seat near Sam. She threw him a shy smile before turning back to her food. Seth looked absolutely pleased with the arrangement as he tore into his hamburger with enthusiasm.

"It's nice out here," Alice said. She leaned back on her elbows. "We should eat outside more often."

"Yeah," Emily echoed. "It's so full of fresh air and stuff."

Ava glanced at me for approval. I shrugged and she smiled. "I like it, too," she said quietly.

The sun felt so good against my wings I stretched them without realizing what I was doing. I glanced up to see Alice watching me. "You're wings are beautiful," she said.

I pulled them back in. "I'm not supposed to do that," I replied quietly.

"What?" she asked.

"Draw attention to his wings," Seth answered with his mouth full. "It's against the integration laws."

Surprised, Alice sat up and several of the girls drew closer. "What else aren't you supposed to do?"

Unused to the attention, I glanced at Ava. She nodded encouragingly. I pulled up several blades of grass and kept my attention on them as they fell through my fingers. "We're not allowed to fly, fight, or train."

"Train," Alice said, shaking her red hair back from her shoulders. "Isn't that what Galdoni do?"

"Yeah," Emily said. "That's like telling my brothers not to play Frisbee."

"Or forbidding us from practicing," Sam said. She ran a hand through her straight blonde hair. "How crazy is that?"

"What's Frisbee?" I asked.

They all stared at me. "What kind of a life did you live?" Sam asked. All the stares turned to her.

I shrugged, unable to come up with an answer. "At least it got me here." I looked at Ava. She smiled at me and I returned it.

"What's going on?"

I grimaced at Brayce's grating voice. The birds flew away as his shadow hovered over our group.

"It's fitting," he continued. "The birds eating with the birds."

"Birds eating with birds," Tavin parroted with a laugh.

My muscles tensed. I didn't care what he said about me, but Ava was present. I wouldn't stand by and let him insult her. My hands clenched. Seth grabbed my arm.

Before I could act, Alice stood with her hands on her hips. "Those birds you scared away have more intelligence in their little wing feathers than you do in your entire body."

Brayce's mouth fell open. Tavin and Manny laughed until he silenced them with a look that threatened death.

"That's right," Amelia, Alice's second said. "So use your two brain cells to go back to the school."

Brayce looked from the cheerleaders to Seth, then me. I could see the rage burning through him, but he was outnumbered. It didn't take a Galdoni to see that he was afraid even though they were girls.

"You better watch yourself," he told me.

"You mean watch me eat with beautiful girls on a sunny day?" I replied.

He stormed away. Tavin, Manny, and the hulking Chad followed.

A bell rang, signifying five minutes before the end of the lunch hour.

"We'd better get ready for the assembly," Alice said, rising. The rest of the cheerleaders stood with her. She smiled at Ava. "You want to come?"

Ava gave me a questioning look. "Go ahead," I told her. "I'm not a huge fan of assemblies. Too many people in one place."

She nodded with a smile. "Catch you later?"

"Definitely," I replied, warmth spreading through me at her look.

She hurried with the other girls toward the gymnasium.

"Alice!" a boy called. I looked up to see four members from the football team waiting for them.

One put an arm around Ava's shoulders. She didn't shrug him away like I expected. Instead, she smiled up at him when he opened the door for her.

Jealousy filled me. I wanted to break his arms for touching her. I wanted to make him suffer for bringing a smile to her face. I should have been there instead.

"Reece, you alright?" Seth asked. He looked from me to the students disappearing inside the gymnasium. "Dude. That's Randy Jenkins. I didn't know he liked Ava." He glanced up at me and his eyes widened. "Oh."

I met his gaze. "Don't say 'oh' like it means something."

Seth shook his head. "I didn't realize you liked her like that. She and Randy hang out but it's probably just—"

"She should hang out with him."

Seth stared at me like I was insane. He blinked at me owlishly and tried to smooth down the cowlick at the front of his short red hair. "What?" he asked after a moment.

I shrugged and pretended not to care. "She should hang out with him. He's probably a good guy."

His eyes narrowed slightly. "And you're not?" he asked.

"I'm a Galdoni," I stated as though that should answer everything.

He shook his head. "Don't settle for that, Reece. Being a Galdoni doesn't make you bad or good. It's just who you are."

I looked at him out of the corner of my eye. "It makes me a trained killer. She doesn't need that in her life."

"How do you know what she needs?" he pressed.

I sighed. "She needs normalcy, Seth. She doesn't need the kind of crazy that comes with a Galdoni."

"Do I need to remind you that she *is* a Galdoni?" he pointed out.

I shook my head. "She's different. You know that as well as I do. She wanted a normal life and she deserves one." I gritted my teeth, but the words slipped out anyway. "Now if I can just tell my heart that."

"Why?" Seth asked quietly.

"Because I want to break that Randy guy's arms," I replied.

Seth laughed. "See; I told you that you like her!"

I tried to punch his arm, but he dodged out of the way and grabbed our trays. "I'll see you after the assembly, Romeo," he called back with a grin.

I shook my head and watched him go. As much as I tried to pretend I was fine, the image of Ava and Randy walking inside the gym together was killing me. I didn't know what to do. I was worried that if I saw Randy again, I might actually kill him. If I saw Ava, I wasn't sure what I would do.

I broke the rules and flew to the roof of the gym. It was a new building with wide windows and a lower roof that transitioned to the higher roof with another set of windows. If I pulled up on the ledge, I could peer down at the crowd of students below. Instead, I sat with my back against the wall and tried to clear my thoughts. I could hear shouting inside as the cheerleaders rallied the students for the football game that weekend. I buried my head in my hands.

Chapter Eight

Lights flashed. I knew the Arena was going on. I wanted to be there, to see the fight and participate in it. Galdoni were living and dying for honor, guaranteeing their spot in the heavens. I tried to picture them. They would be wearing the masks and armor of warriors, gold, silver, and bronze. I wondered what armor I would be given for my first turn in the Arena. It was too bad I had so long to wait. Galdoni weren't allowed to fight in live matches until they were at least sixteen. I had two more years to go.

I couldn't decide if I wanted to fight because it was the thing to do, or because it was better than sitting in my little cell picturing how I would die. Death was inevitable. Death was guaranteed. I wasn't afraid of death. At least, that was what they told us. Maybe all I wanted was to get to the Arena and prove to myself once and for all that I could face it.

The screams in my head became real. I blinked and realized I was still sitting on the roof of the gymnasium with the second wall of windows at my back. I frowned. There should be shouts and cheers, not screams. I pulled up and looked in the high windows. My heart stopped.

A man in a black suit flanked by two Galdoni stood in the middle of the gymnasium floor. He held a gun and was pointing it at the students and teachers who were screaming and cringing together on the stands.

The Galdoni on either side held knives and swords. Thank goodness for Galdoni honor, even it if was antiquated. Our training was hard to push aside. Honor that dictated death by a sword and giving death by a blade would probably save lives today because there was only one gun instead of three.

"Where's the female Galdoni?" the man demanded.

86

I found Ava in the crowd. Her friends and the boys who had been with them were pressed around her, hiding her wings from view. The action gripped my heart in a fist. They were risking their lives to protect her.

I shoved my wings back hard and rose high into the air. I flattened my wings to my sides and dove toward the windows that spilled light onto the gymnasium floor. I punched my left fist forward at the last minute. The glass shattered and I plummeted toward the floor.

I didn't use my wings to slow me. Instead, I landed on the man with the gun with the full force of my momentum. He crashed to the ground and the gun slid away.

"Kill him!" a Galdoni yelled. They were on top of me before I could gain my senses again.

"Reece!" I heard Ava shout.

I rolled to the right, breaking free of the punches and kicks. The fiery slice of a knife blade down the arm I held over my face let me know how close I came to getting blinded. I jumped up and grabbed the Galdoni's knife arm, chopped his elbow so that his arm bent, and spun toward his body. I drove my elbow into his stomach; his breath left him in a rush. I slipped my right ankle behind his left one, and swept his legs out from under him. He fell to the ground and the force of my weight against my elbow drove the air from his lungs. I spun in a crouch and slammed a haymaker into his jaw.

I turned in time to avoid the second Galdoni's knife. He lashed out with his short sword. Pain traced my cheekbone as the tip of the blade cut deep. His momentum spun him to the left. I took advantage of it and punched him behind the ear followed by a two-handed slam to the ribs. He stumbled forward and dropped the sword, but he held the knife tight when he turned back, fire in his hate-filled eyes.

I could hear sirens in the distance. Help was on its way. I had never fought a grown Galdoni before besides Lem, but that was just practice. I could hear Lem's words in my mind.

"Use the thing you have that they don't. They might be bigger, faster, stronger, or just plain meaner, but you have something your opponent is lacking. Find that weakness and use it against them." I pushed my wings down.

"Running away?" The Galdoni called. He lifted his huge pale wings and rose as well, chasing me toward the high gymnasium ceiling. I fainted to the right, then tucked my wings and dove left. He followed close behind. I felt the tip of his knife brush the feathers of my right wing. Screams echoed up from the students below. I tucked my wings tight and spun left. He followed close behind.

"Give up, boy," the Galdoni said in a growl. "You're dead already."

If he killed me, the students would be left unprotected. They wouldn't give up Ava. It would be a massacre. I had to stop the Galdoni. I couldn't shake him. He was behind me, a dangerous place because if he gained even a breath on me he could cut one of my wings and watch me fall to my death. I had to shake him.

"Use his weakness," Lem's voice echoed.

I gritted my teeth and dove toward the gymnasium floor. Amid shouts and screams, I pulled up at the last second, dodged his attempted swipe at my chest, and forced my wings down hard once more. I shot up toward the gymnasium ceiling. A glance back showed my attacker gaining momentum.

"I'm losing patience," he called, his voice rough with anger.

I was close to the ceiling. I would have only one chance.

I flipped backward at the last second before I smashed into the ceiling. I kicked against the ceiling as hard as I could and tucked my wings tight. I cut through the air toward the Galdoni faster than he could react. I grabbed his knife hand as I hit him with the force of a bull. We plummeted toward the gymnasium floor. He struggled, but there wasn't time for him to fight free. There wasn't time for anything. The screams of the students echoed in my ears.

We hit the floor so hard I blacked out.

I became aware of shouting and the sound of sirens. Somebody rolled me over.

"There's so much blood," a student said.

"Give him some space," I heard Mr. Bennett say.

"Reece!" Ava called.

I blinked and opened my eyes. Relieved faces peered down at me. Ava dropped to her knees at my side. I sat up slowly, holding a hand to my head to ease the pounding. Hands helped steady me. I glanced at the Galdoni. He was dead, the knife shoved through his ribcage straight into his heart. The other Galdoni was moaning, but someone had tied his arms and legs with jump ropes. The man in the black suit wasn't moving.

"Are you alright?" Ava asked.

I nodded and looked at her.

"Your face," she whispered. She put a hand to my cheek where the knife had cut it.

I touched the wound. "It just a scratch," I reassured her.

Mr. Bennett was busy wrapping his jacket around my arm to staunch the flow of blood from where the sword had sliced it open.

"That was amazing!" Seth's enthusiasm brought a smile to my face. He couldn't stop grinning. "You were like a torpedo! The way you came through that window. It was incredible!" Other students crowding around us echoed the sentiment.

The gymnasium doors flew open. Police officers and Galdoni rushed inside. Kale and Saro met my gaze. I tried to stand, but my knees didn't want to hold. Dozens of hands pushed against me, keeping me upright until I could will strength to my legs.

"I'm alright," I reassured them gratefully.

The students and teachers backed off at the approach of the Galdoni. Kale looked me up and down. "Are you alright?" he asked.

I shrugged and forced my voice to be steady. "Just another day at the Academy."

He cracked a smile and caught me up in a tight hug. "Glad to hear it."

Saro squeezed my shoulder. "You made quite the mess," he said, his tone approving.

"They were looking for trouble."

We turned our attention to the police officers as they put handcuffs on the surviving Galdoni and dragged him out of the gym as he protested. A medical team from the ambulance was loading the man in the suit onto a stretcher; he had a brace around his neck and appeared to be unconscious.

"This your boy?" a police officer with short gray hair asked.

Saro nodded. "Officer Donaldson, this is Reece. Reece, Officer Donaldson." The Galdoni smiled. "Officer Donaldson just transferred to Crosby to work closer with the Galdoni."

We shook hands. He tipped his head to indicate the dead Galdoni. "I'm going to need a statement."

"There's plenty of witnesses," Seth supplied from behind the man.

At the officer's glance, several students held up cellphones. At least half a dozen appeared to have recorded the entire fight.

Officer Donaldson nodded. "We'll need copies of those videos for our records."

"Let's get you cleaned up," Kale said, steering me away as the officer took the students' information.

Ava followed on one side with Mr. Bennett and Seth on the other. Principal Kelley met us outside the door. "I need to speak to all of you first thing tomorrow," he said. I couldn't decide by his expression whether he was angry or just recovering from the shock of having his school attacked by armed assailants.

Saro glanced at me. "You up to coming back here tomorrow?"

I nodded. "This is my school."

Kale smiled and turned back to the principal. "We'll be here."

"Bye Reece, that was incredible!" Seth exclaimed. I couldn't tell if he was happier about the fight or seeing Kale in real life. He couldn't keep the grin from his face.

I lifted a hand and we all raised our wings. Students flooded out the door as we flew into the sky.

"You know we just broke one of the integration laws, don't you?" I told Kale.

He laughed. "I think you broke every one of them back there. Flying, fighting, you name it, it was done. And you saved lives." He smiled. "Maybe the government needs to rethink those laws."

That brought a grin to my face.

***

Ava refused to leave my side as they stitched up my arm and cheek. She held my hand and spoke to me to keep me distracted from what they were doing. I wasn't a stranger to wounds, but I didn't mind in the least. "I was so scared," she said. "I didn't know what to do. I wanted to give myself up because I didn't want anyone to get hurt, but they wouldn't let me."

"You have good friends, Ava," I told her. A brief fire of jealousy surged through me at the thought of the football player's arm around her shoulders. I smothered it with some effort. "I'm glad they were there for you. Friends who stand by you in danger are true friends."

Saro raised an eyebrow from the chair he was sitting in near Kale. "Apparently, you're learning more in that school than I thought. I should have gone."

Kale chuckled. "It would have done you some good."

Saro smiled at the black-winged Galdoni. "I managed to find a few good friends on my own."

Skylar entered the medical ward of the Galdoni Center at that moment with Brie close behind. Skylar sat on Saro's lap and kissed him on the cheek. "Yes, you did."

Ava and I exchanged a smile at their actions. Brie sat next to Kale. He wrapped his wing around her shoulder and she cuddled close to him. "Sounds like it was a rough morning," she said to me.

I shrugged. "Not too bad," I lied to cover the way my insides still trembled at the thought of the entire school in danger. I kept seeing the gunman over and over in my mind. He held his weapon with a sure grip. I didn't doubt that he wouldn't have minded shooting a few students to prove his point.

Brie smiled, oblivious to my troubled thoughts. "Oh, right. Just a day in the life of a Galdoni."

"That's right," Kale replied, shooting me an approving look. "Reece handled himself like a champ. Good thing Lem's been so strict in his training."

My stomach twisted and I met his eyes. "You knew about that?"

"I approved it," he said with a smile. "My boys wouldn't do anything like that without my approval. Goliath checked with me while I was with Saro. He's the one who recommended Lem."

"He's a good guy," Saro admitted. "I had him mistaken once, and he's shown far more character than I ever gave him credit for." Skylar smiled at him.

"Done," Dr. Ray said. "Try to keep that dry." He tied off the gauze wrapped over the wound on my arm. A bandage had been placed over the ten stitches along my cheek. It already itched. I reached up a hand and he swatted it away. "You really don't want those redone."

Kale grimaced as though he had experienced something similar. "Trust the doctor. Give yourself a break."

"Like that will happen. I've never known a Galdoni to take a break," Brie said; everyone laughed, including Dr. Ray with an anguished chuckle.

"There are a few things Galdoni could learn from humans, like how to relax," the doctor said.

Kale laughed. "I hope that never sinks in, Doc. You'd have a bunch of Galdoni too lazy to fly."

"At least my staff could get a break," Dr. Ray replied good-naturedly.

Ava's hand tightened in mine as I stood up. I put a hand to my head to steady the suddenly spinning world.

"You alright, Reece?" Dr. Ray asked with concern.

I nodded. "Just hit the ground a bit hard. I think I'll take you up on that rest."

He nodded. "I'll have my staff check on you every four hours because you've shown some concussion symptoms."

"Thanks, Dr. Ray," I told him.

Ava and I walked slowly to the elevator. I would rather have flown or taken the stairs, but given my disorientation and the fact that we were on the third floor and had to reach the ninth, I didn't want to risk ending up under Dr. Ray's care again in under ten minutes. I figured he would appreciate my foresight.

Ava pressed the up button. A beep sounded and the door opened. We both hesitated. I looked at her. "Is this your first time in an elevator?"

She nodded. "Are you nervous?" She sounded embarrassed to ask.

I stared at her, amazed by how green her eyes were when she was worried. The way she looked up at me made my heart slow and I almost forgot to breathe. I wanted more than anything to lean down and cover her lips with mine. The impulse was so unexpected and surprising that I nearly did it. I stopped and reminded myself very severely that actions completed under concussion symptoms needed to be very closely monitored. "Definitely. Enclosed spaces aren't my favorite."

She smiled as if relieved I was just as nervous as she was. We both stepped inside. I pressed the button for floor nine. The doors closed and the box gave a little jolt. Ava's hand tightened in mine. I wrapped an arm around her shoulders. The back of my mind pictured the action eliminating the same thing the football player had done. I fought back a smile when Ava leaned against me.

The door opened and we both let out a sigh of relief. Ava looked up at me. We laughed at such a silly victory. She walked with me down the hall.

"I've never been in your room before," she said as if she had just realized it.

The thought of my empty walls and bare room flooded me with embarrassment. "There's not a lot to look at," I admitted. I paused in front of room nine twenty one.

She looked at the number in surprise. "You're right above me." Her cheeks immediately turned red. "What I meant is, your room is directly above mine."

I nodded and pushed the door open. "I thought that was an interesting coincidence, too."

She stepped inside with an expectant smile. The look faded when I flipped on the light and she glanced around. I felt immediately defensive about my bare room and lack of furnishings. Despite Saro's offer to have some more brought up, I had never seen the need. It was fine for me. Now there was no place for Ava to sit unless she wanted to take a seat on the bed. At least I made a point to make it every morning.

"This is, uh, nice," she said, though her tone was confused.

My chest tightened. "You don't need to stay. I'm sure after some sleep I'll be—"

She sat down on the bed. After a moment of staring at the floor in silence, she buried her face in her hands. "Reece, I thought you died. When you fell to the floor with that Galdoni, you both hit so hard and he had that knife, and. . . ." Her shoulders shook.

Shocked, I dropped onto the bed beside her and wrapped my arms around her shoulders and wings. "It's alright," I soothed. "Everything's okay."

She shook her head. "I guess I thought. . . I thought. . . ." She fell silent for a moment. Only the fall of her tears was audible. She took a calming breath and sat up, her gaze vulnerable. "I guess I thought that if I made it to school and lived a normal life, nothing could hurt me." She blinked and looked at me as if I was the only person in the world. Her hands gripped mine tight. "But I realized today that losing you would be more painful than anything I've gone through so far."

Stunned, I tried to speak. "Ava, I—"

She tipped her head up and kissed me. Time stood still. I closed my eyes as her taste and scent flooded through me. I kissed her hesitantly at first, but I couldn't hold back. My emotions got the better of me and I pulled her closer, returning her kiss with the possessive desire that had filled me since I first saw her. I felt her smile against my lips. The action made me smile as well. I sat back.

"Well, I feel better," she said, wiping the tears from her cheeks.

I laughed and sat back against the headboard. She slid so that she could cuddle against me the way Brie had with Kale on the medical floor. I realized how good it felt to have someone want to be so close to me. It was different than the nights I had comforted Ava. Those times she needed me; now I knew she wanted me. I couldn't describe how good it felt to be wanted.

Weariness from the crazy day filled me. My cheek burned where the knife had cut it. Whatever Dr. Ray had injected into both my arm and cheek before he began the stitches was wearing off. I closed my eyes and my head lulled forward.

"Reece," Ava whispered.

I opened my eyes feeling like I was swimming through mud.

"You need to lie down," she said with a gentleness that wrapped me in warmth better than any blanket.

I nodded and felt her pull the blankets free when I moved. She guided me to a better position on the bed and tucked the blanket over me. It was the first time in my life anyone had ever tucked me in. I never knew how safe it felt. I heard her hesitate near the bed.

"Stay," I said softly.

"I probably shouldn't," she replied, her voice reluctant. "The nurses will come to check on you and I'll be in the way, I—"

I turned and caught her wrist. She laughed when I pulled on it gently, guiding her into the bed. I lifted the blanket and she slid beneath it. Her head rested next to mine on the pillow.

"This way if I need help, you'll already be here," I whispered into her ear.

A warm smile spread across her lips. "I can handle that."

I turned so I was on my back. She settled under my arm and rested her head in the crook of my arm and chest, my wings spread out beneath us. I had never been so comfortable.

"Goodnight, Ava," I whispered.

She rose onto her elbow and answered by kissing me on the cheek. She settled back against me again. All I wanted was to stay in that moment forever, but the weariness I had been fighting won. I let out a sigh and allowed the darkness to chase the pounding from my head.

Chapter Nine

After the second nurse woke me up quietly to check on me, I couldn't go back to sleep. I slipped carefully away from Ava, then rose and watched her sleep. She looked peaceful, her head tipped to one side and her black hair brushing across her arm. Her wings were pulled up so that they lay along her sides. I settled the blanket over her better, and smiled when she gave a contented sigh.

I was still a bit dizzy, but without Ava at my side I didn't feel like attempting the elevator again. I walked slowly up the steps to the twelfth floor. I walked across the study center which had been greatly improved since the last Galdoni Center. Computers sat on all of the study tables, and small rooms had been partitioned off for those who needed a quiet place to think. Several of the rooms were filled with beanbags and blankets and had projectors on the walls for movies. The younger students loved to take over the rooms; at this hour, though, the floor was unoccupied besides a lone Galdoni at the end.

When I drew closer, I realized it was Koden, the red-winged boy I had protected during the fight on the children's floor. He had a book and appeared oblivious to my presence.

"What are you reading?" I asked quietly, crossing to the chair where he sat near one of the windows.

He glanced up at me, appearing surprised that someone had spoken. His brows pulled together as if questioning why I was there.

"Your book," I said with a smile. "Is it good?"

He held it up so I could see the title. It was my turn to be surprised; he was reading the Bible. I pulled up a chair. He pointed to a verse that had been underlined. I read it out loud. "For he shall give his angels charge over thee, to keep thee in all thy ways."

I sat back and looked at Koden. "You know we're not angels, right?"

He gave a small shrug, a slight smile on his face. He pulled out a picture from the back of the book and handed it to me. I opened it with some reluctance. It was of an angel with a lamb in its arms. The angel had wings that caught the light of the rising sun spilling through the trees, casting its feathers in shades of red.

I looked from the picture to Koden. He was immersed back in his book, his dark red wings hanging loose on either side of his chair. I stood and slid the picture back toward him. He put a hand over it without look at me. I wanted to say something, but I didn't feel it was my place. I walked to the door that led to the roof feeling confused and anxious, though I couldn't explain why. Maybe I did have a concussion.

The cool breeze brushed against me when I opened the door. I smiled at the scents of dew-laden hay from the farms south of the Center. I closed the door and crossed to the railing. The faintest edge of pink touched the buildings. A siren sounded from the city; another rose to join it, the wailing echoing along the streets. Longing filled me.

I heard the door open and turned to see Skylar. I realized I was in their place. Since she and Saro had become a couple, there was an unspoken agreement to let them have the roof at sunrise every morning. It was their time together. Saro had told me the roof at sunrise was the first time he realized he loved Skylar. The thought filled me with warmth at their happiness.

"I'd better get back," I said, heading toward the door.

Skylar stopped me with a smile. "You don't need to go. Saro and Kale are preparing a statement for the press this morning about what happened at Crosby High."

Trepidation filled me.

She read the look. "Don't worry. As the official Galdoni representative, Kale can stand in for you. He's become really good at working with the media since he brought down the Arena." Warmth filled her gaze. "He wanted to shield Saro from the media as well, but when he went to address the press about Saro rescuing the female Galdoni, Saro was determined to be at his side. He said Kale shouldn't have to handle everything alone. They've become quite the team." The pride in her gaze spoke even more than her words. She was proud of them, of everything they had done and who they were.

She walked to the railing. "What are you doing up here?" she asked amiably.

I hesitated, then told her the truth. "I was listening to the sirens."

She nodded. "There're always sirens down there."

"I wish I could help." The words filled me with such longing I wanted to jump off the building and chase the sirens down. "I want to be like Superman, to protect the innocent, only sometimes I wonder if there really are any innocent." Images of the man with the gun and the Galdoni who had joined him filled me with frustration. Our very existence said that there was evil in the world, people who cheered at the death of others and who had created us for that purpose. As much as I had experienced of the world outside the Academy, it was hard to forget where we came from.

When Skylar glanced at me, understanding filled her features. "Sometimes it's best to give those you meet the benefit of being innocent until they prove otherwise. People might surprise you."

I shook my head. "Growing up a trained killer hasn't helped."

She set a hand on mine. "Reece, you're not a killer."

The gentleness of her words filled me with regret. I blinked back the sudden burn of tears. "I killed that Galdoni in front of all those students. The man probably won't survive, either." I glared at the golden horizon. "I am a killer."

"You saved those students," Skylar replied, her voice firm but warm. "Kale told me what you did. If you hadn't ended the attack, there would be families mourning the loss of their loved ones." Her voice caught. "I know what it's like to lose a family member. You did an amazing thing."

I didn't want to believe it, yet honesty shone on her face. It was easy to see why Saro loved her so much. Her short black and red hair swept back from her cheeks and she smiled at me. "You protected the innocent, Reece. Those students didn't deserve to die, and you kept that from happening. At Crosby High yesterday, you were Superman for them."

"I don't know about that," I replied quietly.

"I do," she said, her voice firm with conviction. "Because of you, every student at the school was able to go home. If you hadn't acted, that wouldn't be the case."

"You make it sound so noble," I said. "I was just doing what I was trained to do."

She shook her head. "You went against your training." At my surprised look, she smiled. "Reece, your training was for self-preservation. Every Galdoni here is covered in scars from learning how to protect themselves. If you were only concerned with protecting yourself, you would have flown away." Her blue eyes glowed with the warmth of the sun.

"Except you didn't. You fought two Galdoni and a man with a gun, putting your own life at risk to save others. Tell me where that applied to your training."

I opened my mouth to respond, then shut it again when I had no answer. For some reason, that filled me with a happiness I couldn't deny. "Thank you," I said, my voice just above a whisper. A thought occurred to me. "Where is Kale and Saro meeting with the press?"

"The welcome center on the first floor," Skylar replied. "Why?"

I smiled. "I just have something to do."

She returned my smile. "I'm glad."

I laughed and jumped off the roof. Joy filled me as the cool morning breeze filled my wings. I tipped them to turn around the building, letting the angle of my wings take me quickly to the ground. I swept them back at the last minute and landed on the ground in front of the main doors.

The receptionist was a Galdoni named Bear with dark gray wings. He was built like his namesake. His presence definitely warned any who came to the Center with the intention of causing trouble to rethink their plans. What they didn't know was that the Galdoni had a tender heart.

The second I set foot in the corridor, Bear grabbed me in a crushing hug. "I can't believe you did that for those kids," he said, his voice a deep rumble through the room. "You saved them!"

I patted his arm before he could crush my ribs. "I was happy to help," I told him.

He stepped back with a look of pride in his eyes. "Who would have thought our young Reece could be so brave?"

Embarrassed, I protested, "I'm sixteen, Bear."

He grinned. "Not too young to save hundreds of lives."

I shrugged. "I guess not."

"Are you looking for the press conference?"

I nodded, but was filled with sudden nervousness. "I think so."

He pointed toward a conference room on the left. "Good luck." He slapped my back with enough force to knock the wind from me.

I stumbled toward the room. When I opened the door, every eye turned to me.

Saro smiled. "There's our boy."

Reporters held out microphones and began to bombard me with questions.

"What were you thinking?"

"Were you afraid?"

"Did you know the school was going to be attacked?"

"Are you and Ava going back to school?"

Kale lifted an eyebrow. I just shrugged my shoulders. He smiled and stood from his seat on the raised platform in front of the reporters. "Let's give the kid a chance to collect his thoughts. He's not used to the meek ways of reporters."

They laughed and backed up so I could join the other two Galdoni on the platform.

"I thought you'd be sleeping," Saro said. He tipped his head slightly with a curious look.

I suddenly remembered Ava. I had left her in my bed and took off. I needed to get back. "I, uh, can't get used to sleeping more than four hours at a time. It makes me feel lazy."

Several of the reporters chuckled.

"What made you fly into the gymnasium?" a man with black-rimmed glasses asked.

I smiled at the thought of Clark Kent from Superman and Skylar's words. "I wanted to protect the innocent from getting hurt."

"Do you feel like you and Ava are also innocent?"

"Ava is," I replied.

A few more chuckles rose.

"Do you worry there will be more attacks?"

The thought hadn't occurred to me. Concern filled my chest. I glanced at Kale. He read my look and took over the question. "We are working closely with Officer Donaldson and the Crosby City Police Department to investigate the reason for the attack. Until we know for certain, security at Crosby High and the other schools with Galdoni has been increased in order to keep all of the students safe."

"And if they come back," I said before I could stop myself, "They'll have to answer to me."

Nods of approval and smiles around the room met my words.

"It's nice to know our students are safe with you around, Reece," a female reporter with short red hair said. She smiled. "My daughter goes to Crosby High; what you did deserves so much more than just gratitude. We are in your debt."

I looked at Kale and then Saro. Both of them watched me, curious as to what I would say. I took a steeling breath. "I think I speak for all Galdoni when I say it is our duty to protect those who are weak. We have been raised with certain skills that enable us to be defenders of the innocent and guardians of justice. Nobody should have to fear for his or her life. Fear should never rule our actions. I will do anything I can to protect the students at Crosby High and keep them safe."

A cheer went up from the reporters. I glanced at Kale. He nodded, and there was something on his face I was surprised to see. Respect. The same look showed on Saro's. He spoke to me under the reporters' excitement. "Who knew you would be so good with the media?"

I smiled. "Not me. I have your girlfriend to thank for that one."

"You spoke to Skylar?" Warmth touched his brown eyes at just saying her name.

I nodded. "She restored a bit of my faith in humanity."

Saro grinned. "She has a tendency to do that."

Kale stood. "We've got to get this boy to school. If you'll excuse us?"

Reporters thanked us for our time before filing out of the room. Kale waited until the last one was gone before he turned to me. "That was well done. I thought you might like to avoid some of the chaos."

"I was going to," I admitted. "But I figured you guys didn't need to handle it by yourselves."

Kale and Saro laughed. "We had it covered," Kale reassured me.

I shrugged. "Just the same, backup can be nice. So how about seeing if I'm still welcome at school?"

Saro nodded. "That might be the harder battle to fight. We should probably get going."

I thought of Ava up in my room. Warmth rushed to my face. "I'll go see if Ava wants to fly with us."

Kale nodded. "I'd recommend it. You'll both be safer if you stick together."

I left the room and waved to Bear on my way out the door.

"You must have made an impression," he called. "I've never seen reporters so happy."

"Call it luck," I replied, pushing the door open.

His deep chuckle followed me out.

I flew to the ninth floor, but when I opened my door, Ava wasn't there. I landed on the balcony for the eighth floor. I remembered at the last second that I didn't have access, but Ava saved me the trouble by opening the door.

"I was wondering where you went," she said.

The smile she gave me stole whatever I wanted to say. I stood speechless, also wondering why I had left.

"I, uh. . . ."

She took pity on me. "Are Kale and Saro flying with us to school?"

I glanced down to see both Galdoni waiting on the grass below. I nodded. "We've got a meeting with Principal Kelley."

"Are we going to get dismissed?" There was true worry in Ava's voice.

"I hope not," I said, and realized that it was true. Somewhere in the time since Ava started at Crosby High, I had begun to enjoy my time there.

She smiled at me and stepped off the balcony. I followed close behind. We both opened our wings at the last second and landed near Kale and Saro.

"Remember the feeling of plummeting to your death only to be saved at the last minute?" Saro asked Kale.

Kale nodded. "Ah, the joys of being young."

I laughed. "Kale, you're like, what, three years older than me?"

He nodded, his arms crossed. "And Saro's two years older than you. Prepare to do a lot of growing up in the next few years." He cracked a smile and Ava and I laughed.

We flew together toward Crosby. It felt great to fly in a group. It was almost like we were a flock of birds heading to the same destination. I pushed my wings harder and glanced back to see the others follow me into the clouds. The sun broke above us. Warmth flooded the air, lighting the clouds like golden waves. I turned my face toward the sun.

"Superman knew what he was doing," I said.

Ava smiled. "Yes, he did."

We tucked our wings and dove toward the buildings. I glanced back to see Kale and Saro do the same. Each had a smile on their face as though they were truly enjoying themselves.

"Reece," Saro called.

I looked back down; Ava grabbed my hand and pulled me to the left in time to barely avoid a building. She smiled at me. "Better get your head out of the clouds."

I smiled back. "I like it that way."

Her smiled deepened. "So do I."

Chapter Ten

We landed at the edge of the school grounds. I glanced back to see Kale and Saro do the same. I wondered if they felt it as I did, the foreboding that came with entering somewhere it was frowned upon to be a Galdoni. I wondered if everything was going to change again. Principal Kelley had been pretty upfront about how he felt regarding Galdoni in his school. Perhaps he had decided the government funds paled in comparison to his students' safety.

"Take a seat," he said as soon as Mrs. Jeffrey showed us inside. She smiled at Ava, but there was something in her gaze when she looked at me before she left. A pang of regret filled my chest when I realized it was fear.

Kale shut the door. "Let me begin by apologizing for the attack. We're working to—"

Principal Kelley cut him off. "Nobody messes with students in my school," he said with such heated passion I could only stare.

Nobody used such a tone with Kale if they were smart. It wasn't that he would make them pay; it was a symbol of respect for all he had done. My hands clenched into fists. Ava reached over from her chair and set her hand on mine.

"Like I said," Kale repeated calmly. "We're working to increase protection for the school and—"

"I don't think we understand each other," Principal Kelley said. He leaned against his desk toward Kale. Saro took a step toward him, but the principal didn't seem to notice as he met Kale's gaze. "Nobody messes with the students in my school and we must get to the bottom of why Ava is under attack. I will do all in my ability to keep both Ava and Reece safe while they are at Crosby High."

Kale blinked. "So you don't mean to dismiss them?"

108

Principal Kelley stood straight. "Why would I do that?"

"The threat," Saro reminded him. "You're not afraid their presence puts the rest of your students in danger?"

He frowned. "If the student was human, there would be no grounds to dismiss them. Why should Ava and Reece be treated differently? They're here to learn and they deserve to do so in a safe environment."

Kale nodded, the beginnings of a smile on his face. "I think we understand each other just fine, Principal Kelley."

Principal Kelley held out a hand. "I approve the security changes you have made here, Kale. We will do our best to stick with them and see to the safety of Ava and Reece as long as they are on our property."

"I'll have additional Galdoni rotated along the perimeter during the school days until we find out who is behind the attack. Patrol cars will increase under Officer Donaldson's supervision, and they will contact you periodically to check on the school's status. Is that acceptable?" Kale asked.

Principal Kelley nodded. "Along with the security guards posted at either end of the school, which I assume will continue indefinitely until the culprit is found?"

Kale nodded.

Principal Kelley stuck out his hand. "Then I think we understand each other exactly. I apologize for my tone earlier, but I take an attack on one of my students as an attack on myself. We need to find out who is behind this as soon as possible. I'm very thankful Reece was able to handle the situation, and I feel that the deadly force he used was entirely necessary. I am also willing to testify to that fact."

"Thank you," Kale replied. "We've had phone calls from students and parents last night and this morning attesting to the same thing."

Surprised, I looked at Saro. He nodded, a smile on his face as if he guessed how the news shocked me.

Saro and the principal shook hands. The bell rang. Principal Kelley nodded at me. "I think you both have class starting, don't you?"

Ava and I nodded and left the office quickly. I fought back a smile as we ran down the hall. "Did you expect that?" I asked her.

"Not at all," she said with a laugh over the sound of our footsteps. "You?"

I shook my head. We both grinned as we took our seats in Mr. Bennett's algebra class. I heard whispers as I crossed to my desk in the back of the room.

"Glad to see you back safe, Reece," Mr. Bennett said.

I remembered him standing above me in the gymnasium asking for the crowd to give me air. I smiled. "Thank you for the help, sir."

"Thank you," he replied.

***

Things had changed. It escalated from the meeting with Principal Kelley. Everywhere I went, students asked about the fight and how I was doing. They showed me videos they had recorded on their cellphones, and first-hand accounts were being shared everywhere I went. The gymnasium was closed from the attack, so Seth and I spent third period lounging in the library with the rest of the class. Coach Andrews told everyone to read about the values of exercise, then left to no doubt enjoy a well-deserved break.

"I can't believe you did that," Sam the cheerleader said with awe in her voice.

I had heard the same statement over a hundred times in the last three hours, but I still didn't know how to respond to it. I went with the safe, "It was nothing."

Sam shook her head. "They were going to shoot somebody if we didn't turn Ava over to them, but nobody wanted to do that. The teachers were trying to protect us, but the guy with the gun said he'd kill them if they moved."

There was terror in her voice. The other students sitting close to us nodded, a reflection of the same fear on their faces. Everyone truly had been scared for their lives; that much was brutally clear.

"I'm sorry you had to go through that," I said.

"But you dove through the window," Sam said. "You took the gunman out, and then you fought those other Galdoni better than any fight from the Arena." She froze, her eyes wide as if she realized what she had just said.

Seth stared from her to me. My insides clenched at the statement, but I tried not to let it show. "They were bad people."

"Yeah," Seth swooped in. "Somebody had to stop them. Thank goodness we have our own Galdoni!"

The students around us nodded.

They escorted me like an honor guard to my next class. By the time I went to lunch, I had answered the same questions so many times I couldn't remember speaking so much. I definitely never had at Crosby High.

The students filtered away to their normal tables in the lunchroom. I spotted Ava at a table near the back with her group of cheerleaders. My heart slowed at the sight of the football players with them. Randy Jenkins, the one who had walked with his arm around Ava's shoulders, sat next to her. They appeared to be in a deep conversation.

I grabbed my tray and shoved the door open to retreat to my usual spot on the soccer field. A few seconds later, I heard a commotion following me. I turned, half-expecting to see Seth running to catch up. My heart skipped a beat at the sight of students pouring out the doors. Each had a lunch tray in their hands and was heading my way.

I sat at my tree and watched in amazement as nearly half of the student body sat down around me. The birds hopped and chirped in the trees, no doubt as surprised as I was to see so many students with food. Ava took a seat next to me and gave me a glowing smile.

"How's your day going?" she asked.

"A bit different than the others," I replied, unable to hide my astonishment at the turn of events.

Students laughed around us.

Alice pushed her red hair back from her shoulder. "Everyone just wants to know how you could be so brave. I think if we had wings like you, we would have all flown away."

112

I was about to brush off the question like I had so many times earlier that day, but I couldn't. The sincerity on the faces around me let me know how much my answer meant to them. They had been scared for their lives; somehow, I had become the source of their safety. Skylar's words whispered in my mind. "You protected the innocent, Reece. Those students didn't deserve to die, and you kept that from happening. At Crosby High yesterday, you were Superman for them."

It was obvious by their expressions that her words were true. I let out a slow breath. "I'm just a student," I said softly. The world fell silent around me. Nobody moved. I could hear the breaths of the students nearby as they listened. "I didn't want anyone to get hurt. I didn't think of the gun or the blades, I only thought that if I didn't do something, somebody I sat with at school or saw in the halls might not be there the next day."

The following part was harder to admit. I looked around at the students, ready to be one hundred percent honest with them and myself. "Galdoni were raised for one thing, to kill. We kill to protect ourselves and to gain honor for the next life." I lifted a hand as a few questions were asked. When silence fell again, I shook my head. "I know that last part isn't true. It was hard for me to accept it; hard for every Galdoni to accept it. Everything we knew was smashed into a million pieces when the Academy was brought down."

I stared at the grass near my tray. The tiny blades looked so simple from far away, but on close inspection, they were intricate and detailed, swaying with the wind instead of fighting against it. "I was floating, drifting without a purpose. The Reece you knew wandered these halls and sat in class because there was no place else to go. It was expected of me, even though so many of you didn't want me here." Voices rose in protest. I looked up with a smile and they slowed. "I couldn't blame you. Who wouldn't want to get rid of the killer that haunted your classrooms?"

I looked at Ava. "But I have a purpose now." I met the eyes of all the students I could. "I promise to protect you. Whatever threat attacks this school, whatever danger threatens your lives, I will do anything I can to make sure you are safe." I gestured toward the gymnasium. "I proved myself then, and I promise you now; you're safe with me. I give you my word."

A few students cheered, and the cheer spread like wildfire. Trays were thrown down and students jumped up, shouting their happiness to be alive. They had been threatened, and they had survived. A smile spread across my face as the cheers rose and the students took up a cry. "Reece, Reece, Reece," they shouted.

Seth pulled me to my feet. The students interlocked arms, jumping up and down like I had seen the football team do before a game. "Reece, Reece, Reece," they cried loud enough for it to echo against the school buildings.

I looked at Ava as we were jostled with the rest of the crowd. She smiled up at me with such pride in her eyes I had to fight back tears. There was love there, love and happiness for what I had done. Energy filled me. I couldn't hold it in any longer. I crouched on the ground, then pushed off with my wings so hard the force rocketed me into the sky.

I flew as high as I could until the circle of students below looked like a speck. I was one of them. I belonged in that ring. I was a student, and I was able to protect those around me. I had a purpose.

I tucked my wings in and dove. Cheering met me on the way down and the circle spread to give me room to land. I spread my wings at the very last second and landed on the grass so hard the ground dented with the impact. Students surged forward. Everyone tried to touch me. They tousled my hair, touched my feathers, and patted my back. I laughed as Seth pushed against them.

"Alright, alright, give the man some room," he scolded. "Even the protectors need protection around here."

"I brought a Frisbee," Emily called. She tossed a strange yellow disc to me. It floated on the air like a bird drifting on the wind. "Throw it," she urged.

The students around us spread out. Everyone was watching me. I glanced at Seth. He grinned. "I can never figure those things out. When I throw them, they go straight to the ground. It's dangerous to play Frisbee with me. Someone might not survive."

I laughed and tried to throw it to him. It curved to the left before heading to the ground. Alice ran over and caught it before it hit the grass. "Tip it up a bit more," she said. "We've played with Emily's brothers so many times we had to practice so we could beat them."

"That was a good day," Emily said with a glowing smile. She caught the Frisbee Alice tossed to her. I began to see how it worked. If given the right angle, the Frisbee could catch the wind and use it to stay up.

Emily threw it back at me and I caught it feeling more confident. I angled my wrist where I felt it should go. When I let go, the Frisbee floated across the heads of the students around us. A tall boy with blond hair caught it near the back. "Alright," he shouted, "Let's play a game!"

Teams were divided, and they taught me the rules to ultimate Frisbee. By the time the bell rang, even Seth was throwing it straighter thanks to some tutoring by Sam which left him grinning from ear to ear.

We walked together back to the school, my arm around Ava's shoulders and the students surrounding us. Seth carried our trays proudly to the lunchroom for disposal despite my insistence that we could take care of them ourselves.

"I get some benefits being your friend, right?" he said over his shoulder.

"I don't see how clearing our trays serves as benefits," I protested.

He tipped his head. "Do you see anyone else doing it?"

Ava and I laughed as he dumped the remains in the garbage and slid the trays onto the pile. He then ducked between us and proceeded to walk with an arm around each of our shoulders to our fifth period history class. A note was on my desk when I sat down. I opened it and read, "There's a party at my place after the game tonight. I'd like you and Ava to be there if you can make it." It was signed from Alice.

I passed the note to Ava as Ms. Stacy began our lesson. Ava read it, then looked at me. I tipped my head in question. She nodded, excitement in her eyes. I looked up to see Alice watching us expectantly from across the room. I gave her a thumbs-up and she turned around with a smile.

***

"You guys coming to the game?" Alice asked when school was over.

"Definitely," Seth replied. He smiled at Sam. Red ran across her cheeks, but she grinned in return.

"I was talking to Reece and Ava," Alice said in annoyance.

Seth looked like he didn't even hear her as he watched Sam. I wanted to tell him that if he stared much longer it was going to get creepy, but I also didn't want to embarrass him.

"I've never been to a game before," Ava said. She looked up at me. "Want to go?"

I had seen my share of games in an effort to live the full student life as Kale had recommended, but I didn't really get the point of guys chasing each other around as someone threw a ball.

"Come on," Alice urged. "It's gonna be a good one. We're playing the Antlions from Perry."

"The Antlions?" I asked.

Seth laughed. "Perry's farm country. You get some strange mascots out there."

"Let's go," Ava said.

I couldn't refuse the pleading in her eyes. "Alright."

"Awesome!" Alice motioned for the cheerleaders around us to join her. "We've got to set up, but we'll see you then!"

Chapter Eleven

"Where are you going?"

I paused outside the school's front doors. Even Brayce's voice couldn't damage the lightness that filled my heart, but it definitely threatened to dull the edge a bit. "To the Center to let Kale know we're going to the game," I said, turning to face him.

For the first time, he was there without his little gang. Brayce's bouncers were nowhere to be seen. Still, I didn't want to risk it. "Brayce, after fighting yesterday, I might not be able to control myself. I—"

He held up his hands. "That's not what I'm here for." He glanced back at the school, then shoved his hands in his pockets uncomfortably and looked back at me. "I need to apologize."

Surprised, I looked at the school also. "Did Principal Kelley put you up to this? Because if he did, it's unnecessary."

Brayce shook his head. "No. This isn't for the principal and it's not for the school. It's for me." He studied the sidewalk below our feet for a moment.

I could tell how uneasy he was with the situation, so I chose to give him the space he needed to collect his thoughts. I sat down on the grass nearby and pulled up a few blades, careful to keep my back to the wall and my face towards him in case he had a change of heart or his gang decided to show up.

After a moment, Brayce shocked me by sitting down as well. "You have a thing for grass?" he asked, his tone curious but also derogatory as if he thought it was strange.

I fought back a smile and let the blades sift through my fingers. "I spent the first fourteen years of my life with nothing but cement floors or sand beneath my feet. Sitting on grass beneath the sunlight and with fresh air around reminds me that I'm not a prisoner anymore. I get to live my own life." My voice quieted. "And I think I just started to realize what that means."

Brayce pulled up a handful of grass, bringing a clump of dirt with it. "My baby brother loves grass," he admitted.

He didn't look up, which was good because I couldn't hide the shock I felt that he was opening up to me.

Brayce kept his eyes on the grass, pulling off small bits of dirt and rubbing it between his fingers. "He always giggles when I set him down on it. He lifts his legs like it tickles, but when I pick him back up, all he wants to do is get back down to the grass."

I blinked, trying to take in the truth. I saw a different Brayce in front of me. Instead of the angry bully who was mad at the world and chose to take it out on anyone he could, I sat in front of a big brother who was proud of his sibling and the funny things he did.

Brayce frowned slightly. "That's my job. The second I get home, Parker is my responsibility. Mom left after he was born, saying she couldn't handle another kid." His eyebrows pulled together. "I guess I had been too hard on her growing up." He ran a hand across his face to wipe away any emotion brought by the words, but a short sigh escaped him. "Parker deserves better."

"It sounds like he's lucky to have you," I said quietly.

Brayce looked up at me, his expression fierce as if he thought I was being sarcastic. I met his gaze calmly. "If I'd had an older brother at the Academy, life would have been a lot easier." I tipped my head in the direction of the Galdoni Center. "As it is, Kale and Saro have sort of become my big brothers. They watch over me and help me succeed when I want to give up. I'd be a mess without them."

"You're a mess anyway," Brayce said, though there was no bite to his words. He watched me, waiting to see how I would react.

I surprised us both by laughing. "Yeah, I am." I shrugged. "What do you expect?"

He grinned, the first I had ever seen from the bully. "I guess you're right."

I chuckled. "I have to admit, I didn't expect anyone to actually attack a Galdoni. That was a real surprise on my first day here."

Brayce's gaze dropped to the ground. "Yeah, uh, sorry about that. I've been an idiot."

I glanced at him. "Why the change of heart?"

He crumpled the clump of grass in his fist. "I realized that if I got shot, Parker would have no one to take care of him when Dad's at work." He looked at me. "I never understood what a hero was until that moment."

"Would you accept that I was just being a Galdoni?" I asked, my tone light.

He shook his head. "Only if you accept that I'm a fool." I opened my mouth and he raised a hand with a laugh. "Alright, that was too easy. What I meant was, none of us humans dared to do anything, yet the Galdoni we've been shunning the entire school year puts his life in danger to save us when he could have flown away." His voice quieted as though the question bothered him. "What makes someone do that?"

"Would you accept that I'm a fool?" I asked.

A smile spread across his face. He stood up. "Fine. We're fools." He held out a hand. I accepted it and he pulled me to my feet. "Thanks for being cool about things."

"You, too," I said, still surprised about the way the conversation had gone. I lifted my wings.

"Hey, Reece."

I paused and turned. Brayce held up a finger. "Don't tell anyone I actually have a heart."

"You're secret's safe with me," I replied.

He nodded with a smile. I flew into the air, unable to stop the answering smile that spread across my face.

***

Sitting in the bleachers surrounded by students who were jostling to sit with us was a new experience for me. Everyone was so excited and by the time the game started, I felt like I had a hundred new friends. I couldn't stop smiling. Ava linked her arm through mine and practically glowed every time she looked at me. I felt like I was flying even though my feet were on the ground.

Seth and several other boys explained the tactics of football as the game began. I began to see the strategy involved. It was a lot more complicated than I had first thought. By the end of the first quarter, we were cheering for Crosby's Nighthawks as loud as the rest of the students. I was really having a good time when halftime came.

Seth walked back from the concessions stand carrying hotdogs and sodas for everyone. Students paid him as he distributed the goods. He handed one to Ava and I. I protested. "I don't have—"

He cut me off. "If I can't buy my best friend and the prettiest girl at Crosby High a hotdog, then what good is our friendship?"

"Besides getting you close to the cheerleaders?" I asked with a pointed look at Sam who had helped him carry the drinks and was distributing them to her friends. She looked back at Seth with a wide smile.

Seth grinned. "There are other benefits."

I laughed. He took a seat next to me while Sam sat on his other side.

Something was happening on the field, but I had my focus on the crowd and wasn't paying attention until I heard my name.

I looked at Ava. She was watching me with a big smile on her face. "Go on," she urged.

"What?"

She laughed at my confused expression. "They want to give you a signed football in gratitude for what you did in the gym. Get over there or you'll miss it."

I stood hesitantly, searching out the small group that stood in the middle of the football field waiting for me.

"Reece, Reece, Reece," the students around me began to cheer.

My heart thundered at the sound of my name from so many lips. I looked down at Ava. "You knew about this, didn't you?" I asked above the roar.

She gave a cute little shrug, the red of her cheeks answering my question.

"Come on down, Reece," Coach Andrews called into the microphone. Principal Kelley stood next to him holding a football, along with several other members of the staff.

I tried to pick my way down the bleachers, but everyone kept reaching up to pat me on the back and tell me thank you.

"Use those wings of yours," Coach Andrews said into the microphone.

I looked at the principal in surprise. He nodded in agreement. I couldn't help the grin that spread across my face. I jumped into the air and pushed my wings down hard to rise above the bleachers. Down below, they shouted my name like I was a rock star or something. I couldn't believe it. Everything felt too good to be true. I was just a Galdoni. Somehow, I had also become one of them.

I landed in the middle of the field next to Coach Andrews. "Where do I get me a pair of those?" he asked. "And do they come in yellow and red so I can wear our school colors?" The students laughed. Talking rose from the other side of the stadium where students and family members from Perry watched the proceedings. I couldn't imagine what they thought of a Galdoni being accepted so readily among the student body.

Principal Kelley took the microphone. "As many of you know, we have had the privilege of working with the Galdoni integration program. At first, there may have been a few struggles," he threw me a smile, "But we got past it. I am proud to say that yesterday, Reece showed courage and selflessness far beyond that expected of any student when he took down attackers at our school and saved the lives of countless students. His bravery is an example to all of us of putting others before oneself and fighting for the good of all."

A cheer went up at his words. Principal Kelley smiled at me. "Well done, son," he said without the microphone. He gave my shoulder a squeeze. "I'm proud of you."

Coach Andrews took the mic. "It is with our great pleasure and gratitude that we present this football signed by the team and coaches here at Crosby High to Reece for his selfless act. Thank you."

I accepted the ball with numb fingers. Everyone was watching me and cheering. It was more than I ever expected. I could barely breathe. Coach Andrews slapped me on the back, always helpful. I carried the ball off the field with Principal Kelley at my side.

When we were away from the spotlight, I stopped and leaned against the back of the bleachers. Principal Kelley paused. "You alright?"

I stared at the football in my hands. "This is too much," I said dazedly.

Principal Kelley smiled. "You deserve it, Reece. You put your life on the line for me, for the coaches, for the teachers, and for all those students out there."

"Not for this," I protested.

He nodded. "I know, and that's why we did it. You didn't care about fame or attention. You were just doing what you thought was right."

I frowned, my thoughts scattered. "I was doing what I knew I could. There's a difference."

"What do you mean?"

I tried to put my feelings into words. "I knew nobody in the gym could stop those Galdoni, but I could."

"Have you fought two Galdoni at the same time before?" Principal Kelley asked.

I nodded, but explained, "Younger Galdoni at the Academy, not full grown adults."

"Have you fought a man with a gun before?"

I hesitated, then shook my head.

Principal Kelley nodded as if he had expected as much. "You didn't know you could beat him."

"Bullets pack a bit more punch than a fist," I replied. I couldn't help the wry smile. "No pun intended."

The principal smiled back. "Reece, you might not feel like you deserve all this gratitude, but they feel like you do." He gestured toward the stadium. "Saying thank you is our way of admitting we were unprepared for the situation and we're grateful there was somebody there with the skills to handle it."

I gripped the ball in both hands, allowing his words to sink in. He waited in silence, for which I was grateful. I finally nodded. "Thank you, Principal Kelley."

"Thank you, Reece, for saving my students." He shook my hand before turning toward the parking lot.

"Where are you off to?" I asked.

He turned so he walked backwards as he spoke. "We're killing the Antlions. They haven't scored since the first drive and we're up forty. I'm going home to have dinner with my wife and daughter."

"Have a good night," I called.

He waved and disappeared between the cars.

Chapter Twelve

I had never been to a party before. Alice lived close enough to the school that everyone walked there after the game. The house was already lit up from the basement to the third floor balcony.

"Wow, Alice, this house is amazing!" Ava told her.

Alice smiled. "Thanks. My dad's in the oil business. He's going to get me a car when I pass driver's ed. I'm pushing for a convertible Mustang."

"Is that a nice car?" Ava asked.

"Best ever," Amelia gushed from behind us. "She wants a pink one with a convertible top."

"And a white leather interior," Alice concluded. "I won't let my smelly brother drive it because he'll get the seats dirty."

Ava and I exchanged a smile. She linked her arm through mine and we walked up the wide steps with the other students. Alice threw the doors open. Music rushed out to meet us. We walked through the tall doors to an entryway with marble floors and two sweeping staircases that circled each side of the room up to the second floor.

Students already spilled out of the kitchen carrying drinks and finger food.

"Awesome party, Alice," Brian, the quarterback from the football team, said.

She threw her arms around his neck and gave him a big kiss. He kissed her back, pulling her to the side as he did so that the rest of us could get by.

"Come on," Sam said, leading the way to the kitchen. Seth followed with a look in his eyes that said he would do anything she asked. She pointed out the food that was available along with an assortment of sodas and punch. "You can get *other* drinks in the pool house," she said in a voice just over a whisper.

Seth glanced at me. "That's okay. Galdoni aren't supposed to drink."

"Oh, right," Sam replied with a wink. "The whole integration thing."

Seth grinned. "More like the whole under-age thing. Getting Reece and Ava thrown in jail intoxicated would be the worst thing for the integration."

Sam laughed as if he had just said the funniest thing in the world. He gave me a wide-eyed look. She grabbed his arm and pulled him toward the backyard. He shrugged at me with a helpless expression and followed.

"He's sure smitten by her," Ava said.

The excitement she felt at being at a party made her green eyes sparkle. I wanted more than anything to kiss her like Alice had kissed Brian. "I think I know how he feels," I said.

She looked up at me. Her smile softened and the glow in her eyes deepened. She put a hand on my cheek. Heat flared where she touched me. "You're amazing, Reece," she said quietly. She stood on her tiptoes and kissed me.

I closed my eyes and kissed her back, slipping my hand through her long silky hair to pull her closer. The feeling of her stole my breath and made me forget where we were. It felt like we were alone in the world, encircled by our wings and the embrace I never wanted to end.

"You guys are so cute!" Emily squealed.

I turned to see the cheerleader and several students watching us from the doorway. A blush ran across Ava's cheeks and she ducked her head.

"Reece, Ava, come check out the pool," Seth called from the back door. "The girls are already swimming!"

Glad for the chance to escape, we slipped through the back door and followed Seth down a set of stairs to the swimming pool set in the middle of a manicured lawn and bushes cut to look like swans.

"This is amazing," Ava breathed.

The lights beneath the pool lit it in colors that changed in time to the music. Students were splashing and laughing. Several had jumped in wearing their clothes from the game, while a few girls had already changed into swimming suits.

"What'd I tell you?" Seth crowed. "This party rocks!" He handed Ava and I cups of punch. "Don't worry," he reassured us. "Sam showed me where the real stuff is. Make sure you don't take anything from the bowl. It's spiked."

"What's spiked?" Ava asked.

Sam appeared at Seth's elbow. "Oh, you're so cute!" she said in response to Ava's question. They wandered away and left us confused.

"I never thought I'd hear Galdoni referred to as cute," I said.

Ava laughed. "Yeah, and two times in the last ten minutes? You better punch someone to save your reputation."

I was in the middle of sipping from the cup Seth had given me. Her words caught me by surprise and I had to take care not to spit punch all over her when I burst out laughing.

She grinned. "First one in the pool?"

"Do Galdoni swim?" Alice asked as she and Brian finally made their way from the kitchen.

I shrugged. "I'm not sure. I've never tried it."

Alice's face lit up. "Then let's have a competition!"

Before I could stop her, she held up a hand and the music quieted as though someone had been waiting for the signal. A man in a black vest handed her a megaphone. I wondered how many others waited on Alice's every need.

"Attention, please," she said into the megaphone. When everyone continued conversing in their groups, she yelled, "Can I have your attention!" Everyone stopped talking. She smiled and flicked her red hair back from her shoulder. "Thank you. We have a competition. Reece, here, has challenged Brian to a race in the pool!"

Everyone cheered.

I shook my head. "Alice, I didn't say I wanted to do that. I've never swam before, and—"

"It's fine," she replied, cutting short my protests. "Because Brian sucks at swimming."

"Hey!" Brian protested.

"Don't fish have wings?" Emily asked from my left.

"That's fins, Em," Alice corrected her with an impatient roll of the eyes. She grabbed the sleeve of my shirt. "Come on, Reece. You'll do great!"

I looked at Ava. She followed with an encouraging expression on her face. "You'll do great," she mouthed.

I hesitated at the edge of the pool. Brian was already pulling off his shirt and pants, leaving him in white briefs. Several of the students whistled.

I couldn't remember how I had gotten into the race. I slipped my shirt over my head, then paused at the silence that fell. I felt the stares of every student on the scars that lined my chest and back. I hadn't been to the Arena, but growing up in the Academy where students fought with real blades by the time they were seven left many opportunities for scars. FH709 had given me a set of three deep scars across my chest from his favorite triple serrated blades. At the Galdoni Center, everyone had scars and so it was no big deal. I saw on the faces of those around me that this was a completely different situation.

A footstep followed by a soft touch on the shoulder heralded Ava. "You can beat him," she said loud enough to tear everyone's attention away.

Brian snorted. "As if," he replied. He stood at the edge of the pool with his hands up and knees bent as if he dove into water every day.

"I may have lied about Brian being a bad swimmer," Alice admitted. "He was captain of the swim team before he got interested in football."

"Oh, great," I replied. "Thanks for telling me."

"You're welcome," she said.

I shook my head and walked to the edge. Ava followed. "Maybe it's like flying," she said, her voice hopeful.

"Maybe," I replied doubtfully.

I lined up with Brian. He grinned and flexed his muscles for the crowd. The girls and a few guys cheered. Alice held up a towel. "On your mark," she said, waving it in the air. "Get set, go!" She threw the towel down and we dove.

The second I hit the water, I floundered for a moment. My wings were quickly water-logged and I couldn't make them respond; then Ava's words sunk in. "Maybe it's like flying," I repeated.

I dove back under the water and pushed my wings like I did when I flew. I shot forward through the warm liquid. The lights danced around me. I could see Brian not far ahead. I pushed harder this time and flew past him. Despite the incredible length of the pool, the wall was coming up fast. I could either slow down, or try something that could turn out to be incredibly stupid. I never was the type to slow down.

I pushed my wings again angling for the bottom of the pool. The second my hands touched, I brought my feet beneath me and kicked while using my wings to propel me up. I broke the surface of the pool and flew into the air, showing the spectators with water. Shouts of dismay along with cheers and laughter met me when I landed on the side of the pool.

Brian's head broke the surface. "Did I win?" he asked.

"He killed you!" Alice exclaimed.

I held out a hand. Brian hesitated, then a grin crossed his face and he took it. Alice threw him a towel. "Nice going," she said.

"That was awesome!" Sam exclaimed. Several other spectators agreed.

"It was like you were flying under water," Emily said with a giggle.

"That's what it felt like," I told her. "It was fun once I got the hang of it."

Ava brought me a towel and my shirt. "Flying under water?" she said.

"It was you're idea," I replied with a grin. "You're next."

She laughed and handed me the towel. I dried off the best I could, but it was a warm night and air drying wasn't such a bad idea. I took a seat with Ava on the lawn chairs that were spread nearby.

"That was beautiful," a girl with green hair gushed.

"It was so graceful," her blue-haired friend agreed.

"Wings would be handy in football," a voice said.

I looked up just as Randy, the boy who had walked with Ava, dragged a chair over and sat down.

"Touchdowns would be a breeze." He gave a wide smile. "Get it? It's because you'd use the breeze."

Several of the girls giggled.

I smiled at Ava. Her eyes twinkled with the lights strung on lines overhead. I wanted to kiss her again. I let out a slow breath, reminding myself that we were in a crowd.

I leaned on an elbow toward Randy. "This may not be socially appropriate to admit, but I wanted to kill you the first time I saw you," I said amiably.

His eyes widened and he sat up; he didn't look scared, just interested. "Why is that?"

"Well," I glanced at Ava who watched us both curiously. "I thought you were putting the moves on Ava. I've never felt so jealous," I admitted. I smiled, "But I know Ava's mine now, so I—"

I saw Ava tense out of the corner of my eye. "I'm not anyone's," she snapped with true anger in her voice.

Surprised, I held up a hand. "I didn't mean it like that, I just meant—"

Ava stood up. "Nobody owns me," she said loud enough that the students across the pool could hear. Silence fell as she stalked across the backyard and into the house.

I looked back at Randy. He shrugged with the same wide-eyed expression as if he didn't know what had happened either. I grabbed my shirt from the back of the chair and hurried after Ava. I ran through the house and caught up to her as she stormed across the front porch. "Ava, wait!" I grabbed her arm.

She turned and hit my hand away. "Don't touch me like that!"

Caught completely off guard by her sudden change in demeanor, I held up my hands. "I'm sorry, Ava. I don't know what I did wrong."

The few students who were relaxing on the steps had the good sense to go inside. Ava leaned her head against one of the pillars. She was crying. I didn't know whether to try to comfort her or leave her alone. My impulses hadn't done well for me so far. Against every longing in my heart, I turned to leave.

"Reece, wait."

The heartache in her voice ate away my doubts. I hurried to her and wrapped her in my arms. "Ava, I'm so sorry. I didn't mean to hurt you. Whatever I said, I take back a hundred times over."

"It's not you, Reece," she said, her tears falling on my bare chest. "It's just. . .it's. . . too many memories," she concluded with a sob.

I led her over to the porch swing in the corner and sat down. She curled up against me, her legs tucked beneath her and her head under my arm so that she rested against my chest. Her dark gray wings spread along her body to chase away the chill of the night air.

I waited until she chose to speak. If it was memories that haunted her, I had enough of my own to know what a torment they could be.

"I just heard it over and over again," she said softly. "She's mine. She's my property. She's my right." She stifled a sob. "Then they would take me. They would. . . hurt me. They had no right." Her hands clenched into fists. "I'm nobody's," she shouted with enough vehemence that the words echoed along the porch.

I smoothed her hair, at a loss for words. Anger built up inside of me. I wanted to find whoever had hurt her and make them pay. They shouldn't have gotten away with it. Nobody should leave a girl trembling in a fear at a touch on the arm or a word spoken without thought.

"I'm so sorry," I whispered, tucking a strand of hair behind her ear. "I didn't know."

"I know," she said, tears still falling. "It's not your fault."

"It's not yours, either," I told her. She kept silent. I could tell that she didn't believe me. I willed her to understand. "Do you remember when you said all Galdoni are killers, and you had hoped I was different?" She nodded without speaking. I tipped my chin down so that it rested on her head. "I told you that you couldn't choose your origin, only what you make of it."

Memories flashed through my mind, boys crying as they learned to stitch their own wounds, knuckles beating against swinging bags, the soft snick of a whip cutting into flesh, the sound of boots walking past my solitary confinement room. "We were created to be victims, Ava," I told her softly. "We were made to be products, me for a society that needed an outlet and a government short of money, you for power-hungry fools who don't understand the meaning of innocence." I took her hand. Her fingers laced between mine, filling me with warmth. "You might have lived through it, but you aren't a result of it," I told her.

She looked up at me with tears in her eyes. "It feels like the same thing," she said.

"You are far more than those men ever knew," I told her. There was an expression in her eyes as if she needed to hear it, to be told the things she had hoped but never dared to truly believe. I told her the things I knew were true. "You are so strong, Ava. You are your own person, brave, defiant, beautiful, and full of grace." I smiled. "Whenever I look at you, I'm filled with such peace and joy because the light that shines from you brings warmth wherever you go. It's as if I'm Superman and you're my sun."

The cheesy analogy brought a smile to her face like I had hoped.

I continued, "Never settle for what they told you to be. You are so much more. You are here because you're a fighter.

You don't give up, and you know there is something better around the corner. Believe in your dreams, Ava, because I believe in them for you. Whatever you want to be or do, you can. You are so amazing." Tears burned in my eyes. I blinked to keep them from falling. "I'm not even worthy of you. I'm a Galdoni with blood on my hands. You deserve so much more. I don't know why you even hang around me."

"Because I love you."

Her reply took everything from me. I could only stare down at her, lost in her beautiful green gaze. I willed myself to breathe, to reply, "Y-you, you what?" I was finally able to ask.

She gave me a smile so sweet my tears broke free. "I love you, Reece."

I shook my head, trying and failing entirely to believe it. I didn't deserve such happiness, such beauty, and such grace. She was so far beyond what I was that I couldn't wrap my mind around her words. "Why?" I whispered.

She set a hand on my cheek. I closed my eyes and put my hand on hers, keeping it there. "Because you're amazing, Reece."

I shook my head without opening my eyes, afraid of the tears that continued to fall, revealing how she had taken my heart and left me bare. "I'm not, Ava. I'm nobody."

"That's not true." When I didn't answer, she said my name. "Reece?"

I would never tire of hearing the sound from her lips. I took a shuddering breath and willed my eyes to open. She looked up at me with such love it was all I could do to meet her gaze. "I'm yours, Reece," she said.

After all she had told me, the words meant more than I love you. I pulled her close and buried my face in her hair that smelled of vanilla and lavender. "I love you so much my heart would break if I didn't say it," I told her. "I think of you every moment of every day. I want to keep you safe and make sure you're happy. You deserve every joy in life, and I will do my best to make sure you have it."

Her arms wrapped tightly around me. I returned the embrace. Her chin tipped up and I kissed her. She was my everything. I would never be the same, and I was glad.

Chapter Thirteen

When we returned arm in arm through the door, students scrambled to get away from the windows. I realized the window closest to the porch swing had been open.

"Why don't you say beautiful stuff like that to me, Brian?" Alice demanded.

The quarterback threw me a bewildered glance; I was starting to suspect that was the way he usually looked around the head cheerleader.

"You two are so romantic," Emily gushed. Ava smiled at her as a beautiful blush ran across the female Galdoni's cheeks.

I called to Alice, "Thanks for inviting us to your party. We've got to get going."

She ran over and gave us each a hug. Seth looked perfectly content to stay sitting on a kitchen stool with Sam on his lap forever. I had never seen him happier. I waved and he returned the gestured. "Good for you," I mouthed. He grinned in response.

Ava and I walked together to the front door. Alice and the other cheerleaders along with the friends we had made at the party called goodbyes and wishes to get together soon. We lingered at the bottom of the front steps, reluctant to leave. It was the beautiful end to an amazing day.

"Look out!" someone shouted from the lawn, jerking me back to reality. Screams followed.

My heart skipped a beat at the sight of four Galdoni landing on the grass. My muscles tensed, ready to defend those I cared about. I pulled Ava behind me for safety.

"Call nine-one-one," I shouted over my shoulder.

Screams went up as students realized what was happening.

"Give us the girl and nobody gets hurt," a Galdoni with thick black wings said.

"You aren't getting past me," I replied, standing at the base of the stairs.

"You better just leave if you know what's good for you, boy," the black-winged Galdoni growled.

"I was going to say the same thing to you," I replied in the same tone.

A blond-haired Galdoni with gauntlets laughed. "We're going to enjoy this."

"Go into the house," I said to Ava. She turned and ran up the stairs.

A brown-winged Galdoni jumped in her way.

"Leave her alone," Seth yelled from the porch.

"Yeah," a dozen other students shouted.

The Galdoni looked back in surprise. I dove at him, barreling him over with the distraction. Ava ran past the Galdoni into Alice's arms. I glanced up in time to see the girls help her into the house. The football players barred the way so the Galdoni couldn't follow.

I gasped as gauntlets drove into my ribs. I turned with the blow and pulled the Galdoni into my fist. He stumbled backwards. The hiss of a sword through the air met my ears. I ducked and spun, knocking the legs out from the armed Galdoni. I lashed out with a haymaker when I completed the spin, slamming it into the jaw of the blond Galdoni.

"You'll pay for that, kid," a Galdoni growled.

Pain flared along my side when the sword struck home. I bit back a cry and kicked the kneeling Galdoni in the head. He fell over with a yell of pain. I could feel blood seeping from the wound. I blocked a punch, answered with another one that was also blocked, ducked under a kick, then jumped and used my wings to spin me in a tight kick that connected with the gauntleted Galdoni's head. He fell to the ground.

"I've had enough of this," the black-winged Galdoni growled. He attacked with a set of knives. I stumbled back under the onslaught.

"Reece!" Seth yelled.

I glanced up in time to see him throw a fireplace poker in my direction. I caught it out of the air and turned back, using my momentum the way Lem had taught me to increase the power of my swing. The blow caught the black-winged Galdoni's arm with a loud crack. He yelled and dropped one of the knives. I was about to grab it when the Galdoni with the sword stumbled over to us, his blade wavering in the air.

"Kill him!" the black-winged Galdoni shouted, clutching his broken arm to his side.

The command seemed to ignite a fire under the other three. They attacked in a group. Though I could tell my blows had shaken them, they were ferocious and relentless. I was pushed back to the steps as I blocked punch after punch and ducked another swipe of the sword intended to take off my head.

"Reece!" Ava yelled.

I looked up in time to see the black-winged Galdoni's hand come down. Something hit my shoulder so hard I stumbled back on the steps. I stared at the knife protruding from the right side of my chest.

Adrenaline pounded through my veins. I let out a yell and gripped the fire poker with my left hand. I parried a swipe of the sword, then drove the poker into the first Galdoni's stomach. I blocked a kick with my right forearm and slammed the poker into the next Galdoni's ribs. I fought to breathe. Black spots danced in my vision. I ignored them.

Ava's safety and the safety of the students behind me were at stake. The Galdoni wouldn't get through me.

"Reece, look out!" Randy shouted from the porch.

I turned in time to block a kick from the black-winged Galdoni. I punched his broken arm. He let out a yell of rage and slammed his fist into the knife protruding from my shoulder. My knees gave out at the pain and I fell to the grass. Two Galdoni jumped on me.

"Reece!" Ava cried.

I heard the pounding of footsteps as students raced down the stairs to my rescue. They would be killed. There was no doubt about that. The thought gave me the strength to act. I kicked and sent the first Galdoni flying over my head. When I rolled to my hands and knees, the other Galdoni pinned me.

My body used the muscle memory from my practice with Lem. I grabbed the Galdoni's left hand and rammed my shoulder against him, throwing him onto his back. I rolled across him to a crouched position and drove two haymakers into his jaw. I followed up with a two-fisted slam to the chest that brought a yell of pain from me and broke at least a few of his ribs, if not his sternum. I left the Galdoni gasping on the ground.

The blonde Galdoni and the black-winged one were charging up the stairs after the students and Ava. I gathered what strength I had left and dove into the air. It about killed me to bring my wings down with the knife through my shoulder, but the force propelled me forward. I landed on the step just ahead of the Galdoni.

"Leave them alone," I growled.

The fury in my voice checked both of them in their tracks. They glanced at each other.

"We have our orders," the black-winged Galdoni barked at his comrade.

Sirens sounded in the distance. For the first time, fear showed on both Galdoni's faces. I wondered what waited for them if they were brought in.

"Next time, you won't be the only casualty," the black-winged Galdoni threatened.

"I'll be ready," I replied calmly as though I wasn't on the verge of collapse.

He grabbed the brown-haired Galdoni under the arms. The blonde Galdoni picked up the one with the sword. "Let's move," the black-winged Galdoni commanded. They took off into the night sky.

My knees gave out. Students rushed forward and caught me. They eased me down onto the steps.

"Reece," Ava said, kneeling beside me. "We've got to get you to the hospital."

"I'm alright," I protested weakly. "We've got to get back to the Center. Kale needs to know what happened."

"You're in no shape to fly," she said, her voice shaking.

I gritted my teeth and stood back up. Silence and a hundred anxious faces watched me. I met Brian's gaze. "Can you make sure everyone gets home safely?" I asked the quarterback.

"I will," he promised.

I turned to Seth. He watched me with concern bright in his eyes. "When the cops show up, give them this." I pulled the knife from my shoulder. It had seemed like a good idea at the time, but the pain that pulsed from the wound and the blood that started to flow said I probably should have left it there. I handed him the knife and gave him a weak smile. "More benefits of being my friend?"

"It just keeps getting better," he replied, his eyebrows pulled together worriedly. "You gonna be okay?"

I nodded. "Galdoni were made to bleed, remember?"

I raised my wings. It hurt more than I wanted to admit. Ava stood beside me, her green eyes bright with unshed tears. "Tell the cops everything," I instructed the students who watched us. "They'll make sure you're safe. If Officer Donaldson gets here, let him know Kale is going to need to talk to him." Several nods followed my words.

Students huddled against each other. Boyfriends held girlfriends in protective embraces, girls clutched each other's hands, and boys stood in groups. It ate at me that they probably would have had a fun evening of partying if we hadn't shown up. I glanced at Ava and saw the same sadness on her face.

"Let's go," I said quietly. I forced my wings down and rose into the sky. I lifted a hand in farewell. A hundred hands responded. We turned our wings and headed toward the Galdoni Center.

"Think they'll be safe?" Ava asked.

"They're safer without us there," I replied. The black spots in my vision were growing. I couldn't think past a humming sound that filled my mind.

"Reece? Reece!" Ava shouted. She grabbed my arm and pulled me up in time for me to miss slamming into a rooftop.

I forced myself to focus, pushing all of my energy into flying. Ava kept a tight hold on my arm. By the time we reached the Center, her touch was all that kept me in the air.

I crash landed on the third floor balcony. Ava put her hand to the print reader. I could barely lift my head to see tears streaming down her face. The door buzzed open.

"Help!" she called. "Anyone, please help me!"

I heard footsteps running toward us, then female voices spoke. I recognized Skylar's among them. She knelt down next to me. "Reece, can you hear me?"

I forced my eyes open. "Tell Kale Donaldson needs the knife," I mumbled.

Skylar's brow creased with worry. "Reece, I don't know what you mean. We need to get you to Dr. Ray. Can you stand?"

I shook my head, unable to even think about the effort it would take to do so.

Heavier footsteps ran toward us. The door was pushed open. Light flooded out. I squinted and relief flooded me at the sight of Kale and Saro. Kale dropped to his knees next to me. "Reece, what happened?" he asked, checking me over quickly. When his hands came away damp with blood, his face paled. "Get Dr. Ray," he called.

"He's here," Skylar replied breathlessly, running back to the door.

Dr. Ray pushed through to the balcony and knelt next to Kale.

"He's losing blood fast," Kale told the doctor.

"Carry him to a bed," Dr. Ray ordered.

I gritted my teeth, but a yell escaped me anyway when Kale and Saro picked me up as gently as they could.

"I'm so sorry," Kale apologized as they settled me on the bed Skylar hurriedly pushed over.

Dr. Ray pulled back my shirt to reveal the wound in my shoulder. I could feel the warm blood flowing down my arm.

"His side," Ava said, her voice tight. "One of the Galdoni had a sword."

"Galdoni?" Kale repeated in shock.

Ava's reply was drowned out by the humming sound. I watched Dr. Ray's eyes widen when he moved the shirt from my side. He called out orders, but I couldn't hear them.

Saro knelt by the bed. He was speaking, his gaze on my face. I tried to hear him, but I was too far gone. The dark spots in my vision grew bigger until I couldn't see him anymore. My world filled with silent night.

Chapter Fourteen

A steady beeping sound awoke me. I was aware of oxygen rushing into my nose in a steady, cool stream. I tried to remember where I was and what had happened. Everything was a blur. I remembered a pool, swimming through water as if it was air. There had been laughter, followed by screams. My eyes flew open.

"Ava!" I called, sitting up. I gasped at the pain that flared so strong through my shoulder and side I couldn't breathe.

Strong hands eased me back down. When the pain diminished, I was able to focus on the face above me. Kale gave me a concerned smile. "Ava's safe. You've got to take it slow."

I shook my head. The movement made the room spin. "But the Galdoni. . . ."

Kale nodded. "They got away, but you protected the students. The other Galdoni from the school has awoken and is in interrogation. We'll find them."

"Is Ava safe?" I asked, unable to push past the thought of her in trouble and afraid. There were too many Galdoni. They were so strong. I tried to force my mind to focus.

"She's at school," Kale said. When I tried to sit up again, he held me down with one hand on my chest. It shouldn't have been so easy. "Trust me," he said. "She's okay. I doubled security at Crosby High and Lem's in charge of her safety. She'll be okay."

Kale's cellphone rang.

"They won't hesitate to hurt students," I said as he answered it. "They said there would be more casualties—"

Kale's face washed pale. He rose quickly. "I've got to go. Stay here," he said before he ran out of the room.

Ava. It could only mean Ava was in trouble. The thought propelled me to action. Every movement hurt. I clenched my jaw and sat up; the pain through my side forced a cry from between my gritted teeth. I pulled the IV from my arm and removed the oxygen tube from my nose. By the time I stood, the world was reeling again.

I found my clothes folded neatly on a chair in the corner. I eased out of the hospital gown and put them on with the least amount of pain I could manage. The thought of Ava in trouble spurred me on. It hurt too much to pull on my socks, so I left them and slipped my feet into my sneakers.

I glanced down the hall. There was nobody in sight. Something really bad must have happened. I ran for the balcony, pulled the door open, and fell over the edge.

I should have thought it through a bit better. My wing didn't want to respond with the swelling in my shoulder. I plummeted toward the ground. Three stories sure went by quickly. A yell tore from my lips as I forced my wings to move. They caught the wind. Tears filled my eyes at the pain. I swooped low over the grass and pushed down. The wind carried me above the trees.

I don't know how I made it to the school. I nearly ran into the doors and shoved them open with my good shoulder. Mrs. Jeffrey was gone from the front desk. Adrenaline filled my veins. I ran down the hall toward Ava's English class. When I yanked the door open, twenty-six pairs of eyes turned to me. I spotted Ava on the far row. Relief hit me like a wall.

"Reece!" she said, rising. She looked at Alice. They both stared back at me in shock. "Reece, what's going on?"

"We've got to go," I said past the pain-muddled fog that filled my thoughts.

Ava apologized to Mrs. Simmons and hurried out the door. Alice came with her.

"Reece, how are you even here?" Alice asked.

I shook my head. "Something's wrong at the Center. Ava's not safe. We've got to leave."

Alice nodded at Ava. "You'd better get going." The head cheerleader touched my arm. "Be careful, Reece. You've been through so much."

"Thank you, Alice," I replied, touched by her concern.

Ava ducked under my good shoulder as if she could tell I was moments away from collapsing. We hurried back up the hall. "What's going on?" Ava asked, her voice tight with worry.

I shook my head. "I don't know, but whatever it was sent Kale running to help." I looked down at her and my steps slowed. "I thought it was you. I thought. . . ."

"I'm alright," Ava reassured me as if she knew how badly I needed to hear the words.

I could barely get my mind to believe it; everything was wrong. I couldn't concentrate.

"Reece, I'm okay." Ava stood on her tiptoes and kissed me.

Strength flooded me at her touch. I kissed her back, letting her feel the relief that flooded me at seeing her unharmed. I stepped back and caught her hand in mine. "Let's go."

By the time we reached the Galdoni Center, my mind had cleared enough for me to know I had jumped to conclusions. Perhaps Kale's emergency had nothing to do with Ava. Maybe whatever pain meds Dr. Ray had given me had messed with my thoughts. Galdoni didn't do well on any type of medication. Though with the fiery agony that throbbed from my shoulder and side, I wouldn't have refused a little help. I could tell by the way my clothes stuck to me that both wounds had been reopened by the flight.

We landed on the ground floor because I couldn't force my wings to take me any higher. Ava held open the door.

Bear rose from behind his desk at the sight of us. "Reece, what's going on? I've had a ton of phone calls for you."

"Is Kale down here?" I asked, leaning heavily against the desk.

"He's holding a meeting in room four." He paused and took a better look at me. "I'll go get him."

Ava waited silently at my side. Her hand rested on mine; the touch helped to center me.

"Reece?"

I looked up at Kale's voice. He and Saro hurried up the hall behind Bear. Kale glanced from me to Ava. "What's going on?"

"What happened?" I demanded.

Kale looked at Saro. The gold-winged Galdoni answered. "The Galdoni we captured from the school escaped."

My hope that whatever had happened didn't endanger Ava vanished. "He's our only lead," I said. "Without him, there's no way to track down whoever is behind the attacks. We're vulnerable."

Kale nodded. "We're with Officer Donaldson now working on our next step."

"We have to do a broadcast." The humming sound was returning. I forced my thoughts to focus. "The students at Crosby High are in danger as long as whoever is behind these attacks thinks Ava is there. We have to broadcast that all Galdoni will be pulled from the schools."

Kale held up a hand. "Ava is the only female Galdoni that's gone to school. Crosby High—"

"Is in danger," I said, cutting him off. I knew it was rude, but I couldn't think through the growing hum. "We have to protect the students. They could have been hurt last night."

"Three nights ago," Saro supplied softly.

I glanced at Ava. "You were asleep for three days," she said. There was pain to her words; she had been worried about me.

I took a calming breath to steady myself. I nodded. "We need to make the broadcast. The Galdoni threatened to hurt the students and we know they won't hesitate to do so. We can continue the Galdoni integration later. It's not worth the risk."

Kale set a hand on my shoulder. "Easy, Reece. We'll take care of it."

"Promise?" I asked. The question sounded pathetic to my ears. Blood pounded in my eardrums in time to the throbbing of my wounds. My grip on the counter loosened.

"Do you want to make the broadcast?" Kale asked. "You're quite good at these things."

I wanted to laugh, but my grip on the counter slipped the same time the throbbing became so loud I couldn't hear anything else.

Kale's eyes widened. He caught me before I hit the floor.

***

"Dr. Ray asked me to handcuff you to the bed," Kale said when my eyes opened.

I glanced down at my wrists. They were free.

Kale shrugged. "I told him he was being a bit hasty."

I closed my eyes and let out a sigh. "I overreacted."

Kale's voice was apologetic when he replied, "I should have had Ava taken out of school after the attack, but she insisted. She said she needed the normalcy of her friends and a real schedule. I couldn't argue with that."

I looked at him. "You're not used to arguing with female Galdoni."

He smiled. "As a rule, I try not to argue with any women. Call it self-preservation. For all we know, the Galdoni females are freakishly strong. She may just tear me apart."

We both laughed at the image of sweet Ava taking down the black-winged Galdoni.

I pushed up gingerly. Kale rose as if to help me, but I shook my head. "You've done so much. I wasn't very grateful."

Kale gave a smile that filled his dark eyes. "You were protecting your girl. I would have done the same thing."

"She's not my girl," I replied, remembering our conversation from the party. At Kale's look, I conceded, "Well, she is my girl, but nobody owns a Galdoni."

He nodded. "I can respect that."

I rubbed my eyes. "There's got to be a way to find the Galdoni so we can end this threat and get back to our normal lives."

"You want to go back to school?" Kale asked. At my questioning look, he said, "I know you didn't like it there. Things have changed?"

I nodded. "So much has changed it's not like the same place anymore."

"Or you're not the same person," Kale pointed out.

I studied the blanket over my knees. "A bit of both, I think." I fell silent, thinking through our options. A thought tickled at the back of my mind. I tried to push it away, but it wouldn't leave. I asked Kale quietly, "Has the broadcast taken place?"

"It's scheduled for morning, why?" he asked curiously.

"I think we should cancel it." Surprise lit Kale's face, but he continued to listen. "We know the Galdoni plan to catch Ava when she with the other students, right?"

"That's what it sounds like. Why?" Kale asked.

The thoughts came clearer. "What if we let them?"

"You mean use Crosby High and Ava as bait?" A touch of displeasure hinted in Kale's tone. "I don't think that's wise."

"Hear me out," I said. "It wouldn't be bait if everyone knew what was coming. Principal Kelley said he would do anything to keep his students safe. We can talk to him and see how he feels about it. If it means finding Ava's attackers and putting an end to the threat to both Crosby High and his students, I think Principal Kelley would go for it."

Kale was watching me with an expression I couldn't read. "What do you propose?"

I thought of the banners that lined the school halls. "Prom. It's this weekend and it would be the perfect night for the Galdoni to attack. There are signs advertising it all over the city; they can't have missed them. Dances usually have few chaperones which means less security for the Galdoni to fight. They'd think they were catching us unprepared."

"We'd have to make sure nobody could get hurt," Kale said quietly, thinking it through. "You sure Principal Kelley would do it?"

"If he gives his permission, we'll ask the students to vote. That way everyone will be in on the plan and nobody will be caught in a situation they aren't prepared for."

Kale rose. "Let me clear it with Officer Donaldson. I'll set up a meeting with the principal in the morning if you're feeling up to it."

I nodded. "Thanks, Kale."

He paused, then took a seat again by the bed. "You know, I put you in school so you could live a normal life."

I cracked a smile. "I think this is as normal as it gets for a Galdoni." I shifted in the bed and winced.

He shook his head. Sadness touched his gaze. "I didn't want this for you. You deserve a chance to grow up not fighting for your life."

"I'm not fighting for my life," I replied. At his searching look, I said, "I'm fighting for the lives of others. Galdoni weren't created to do that. And that's what you do, too. We're going against what Galdoni were made for, and so because of that, we are creating our own lives."

He watched me for a minute, his brow creased with thought. When he spoke, it was with a smile. "Maybe I'd better go to that school of yours. It must have some pretty sharp teachers."

"I didn't learn it from them." At his questioning look, I pointed at the shadow in the doorway behind him. "Saro's a pretty sharp teacher also."

Kale rose with a chuckle. "You've been giving Reece life advice?"

A hint of a smile showed in the darkness. "I didn't think he'd actually listen."

Kale grinned. "Well, it's sunk in and he's come up with the best plan we have so far for luring those Galdoni into a trap. If we can get Officer Donaldson and the school on board, we might just be able to make it work."

Saro nodded. "Good to hear it. And to think I was all ready with the Molotovs."

Kale shook his head and patted Saro's shoulder on his way out the door. "I thought you'd be over those by now."

Saro shrugged. "You know what they say. Once a pyromaniac. . . ."

Kale chuckled and walked down the hall.

Saro took a seat by my bed. "How are you feeling?"

I grimaced. "Like I fought Goliath."

He grinned. "I know how that feels." At my surprised look, he nodded toward me. "About like that."

I wanted to laugh, but it hurt too much. I settled for smiling. "Was Kale upset that I jumped to conclusions this morning?"

"Not at all. We both realized it had been reckless to let Ava go back to school. You did the right thing." He gave me a sympathetic look. "I just wish you would have asked me to get her instead of flying over there half-dead."

I shrugged. "Half-dead, mostly alive. I'm more of a cup half full kind of guy."

He chuckled. "Since when?"

"Since I met Ava," I said honestly.

He smiled at that. "I know exactly what you mean. My life started over again when I met Skylar."

"Do you worry about losing her?" I couldn't help it. The Academy had never prepared me for love. We had been trained to shun all relationships, to not even befriend the other Galdoni because they were our enemies. When like wasn't an option, love was far from plausible.

Now it filled my every waking moment, and thoughts of Ava chased through my dreams. All I wanted to do was hold her, and the thought of her in danger set me on edge. I couldn't protect her enough.

"Of course," Saro admitted. "It's my greatest fear. Why do you suppose they never taught us about love at the Academy?"

"Because love is an attachment," I replied.

He nodded. "But it's so much more than that. Love gives you something to fight for. It focuses your energy and gives you drive. What's the worst thing that could happen at the Arena? Galdoni who refuse to die." He nodded at me. "Bleeding to death from wounds like those happened a lot there because we had no reason to keep living."

"You did," I said quietly, remembering the wound on his side.

He gave a wry smile and nodded. "I did out of spite. I definitely didn't love Blade." The thought made him laugh. "But I loved the thought of getting even. Revenge can be almost as strong of a drive, which is why it's so dangerous."

Something about his tone caught my attention. I watched him closely. "Were you driven by revenge after the Arena fell?"

He nodded, his gaze on the flashing monitor at my side. "I wanted to make the man pay who gave me my scars." He rubbed his chest. "Sometimes letting go can be as powerful as getting even."

"If someone hurt Ava. . . ." My hands clenched into fists at the thought. Adrenaline surged through my veins. I wanted to tear the IV out of my arm and make sure she was alright.

Saro set a hand on my fist. "She's alright, Reece. Calm down. Breathe."

I closed my eyes and willed myself to listen. The sound of my heartbeat on the monitor slowed. I took a deep breath and let it out. "Sorry," I said, opening my eyes again. "I think I need to punch something."

He chuckled. "I'll tell Goliath to be ready."

"Reece?"

Everything fell away at the sound of Ava's voice. She rushed to the bed, her gray wings like graceful shadows in the dim room. "Kale told me you were awake."

"Sorry I scared you," I apologized.

She gave me a hug, careful not to touch my wounds.

Saro stood and gave a silent wave. I returned it with a grateful smile. He disappeared through the doorway.

Ava kissed me, her lips warm against mine. I pulled her onto the bed so she could lie by my side. She pillowed her head on my good shoulder. I turned slightly so I could see her soft features. I tucked a strand of her long black hair gently behind her ear. "You're so beautiful," I whispered.

She smiled. "What kind of drugs is Dr. Ray giving you?"

"I'm serious," I replied, smiling down at her. "You are the most beautiful thing I've ever seen. And it's not the drugs talking." I closed my eyes and took a breath, then forced them open again. "But Dr. Ray must have been serious about keeping me in this bed because these sedatives are really hitting home."

She brushed the blond hair back from my forehead, then kissed me gently. "You need your sleep."

I shook my head. "I don't want to miss a minute with you."

"I'll be here when you wake up," she promised.

"T-tell Dr. Ray I need to be alert tomorrow. . . to meet with Principal Kelley."

"I will," she said with a fond smile. She kissed me again.

I fell asleep with the taste of her kiss on my lips and my heart threatening to overflow with love for the girl at my side.

Chapter Fifteen

"I can't tell you how many parents I've had calling," Principal Kelley said when he entered his office. He paused and frowned at me. "Are you sure you should be here, Reece?"

I sat up straighter despite the pain. "I'm fine. Are they asking for us to be dismissed?"

The principal's eyes widened. He looked from me to Kale and Saro who stood behind us, then at Ava who sat at my side. "Are you kidding? They're all calling to thank you."

I glanced back at Kale. "But Bear said he'd been flooded with phone calls."

A smile played around the Galdoni's mouth. "I guess he forget to say what they were about."

Principal Kelley leaned against the desk. "I know what went on at that party, but apparently the students edited the truth a bit, telling their parents that the Galdoni crashed the party, but not that they were searching for Ava. They said you protected them. You're their hero."

I sat back. "They tried to save my life." I remembered the thunder of footsteps on the stairs after I was struck with the knife. The Galdoni would have killed them. "They were the heroes," I said softly.

A smile spread across Principal Kelley's face. He straightened his toupee. "It seems your Galdoni integration program's worked, Kale." He met the Galdoni's gaze.

Kale nodded. "I would be happier if it didn't mean your students were in danger."

The principal nodded. "That we can agree on."

"Reece has a plan that might help us get to the source of the attacks," Kale told him. "But it involves your school."

Principal Kelley took a seat as Kale and Saro explained the plan to him. He listened intently, but worry creased his forehead. "I'm not sure how they're going to feel about it."

I leaned my elbows on my knees. The motion pulled at my side. I gave up trying to find a comfortable position and sat up again. "I think we should let them vote. It may be a way to get everyone out of danger, but it's risky."

Principal Kelley nodded. "We'll call an assembly this morning." He gave me a critical look. "Are you up to speaking? We could turn it over to Kale."

I shook my head. "I'd like to talk to them. I have some things I need to say."

***

The applause that started when I stepped onto the platform in the middle of the gymnasium floor filled me with guilt. It was my fault so much fear had occurred there. They shouldn't be clapping for me. If it wasn't for Galdoni, they wouldn't be in the position I needed to ask from them.

Students stood on their feet. Shouts and cheers heralded from the bleachers. Even the teachers were yelling and clapping. I found Seth in the audience. He was standing with Sam. Both of them clapped and Seth grinned at me. Alice and Brian stood nearby. When I met her gaze, Alice mouthed 'thank you', her eyes bright with tears.

I accepted the microphone Principal Kelley held out. The cheers got louder. I didn't know if I could ask them what I needed to. It wasn't fair. They deserved to be safe.

I glanced back at Ava. She sat with Kale and Saro near the edge of the platform. She looked at me with a smile of pride even while tears shone in her eyes. She knew how hard it was going to be. Kale nodded, the words he had told me in the hall still fresh in my ears.

"Give them a chance. They deserve to know what's going on and have the opportunity to help if they dare. It's a lot we ask of them, but they've already shown a fearlessness and loyalty toward you and Ava that we never expected. The chance to fix this might be worth it."

I took a steeling breath. "Good morning, Crosby High," I said into the microphone. The cheer doubled. I bit back a smile and held up a hand. "Thank you. It means more than you know." The audience quieted down. I had rehearsed a little speech with Kale, but it didn't feel right. I glanced back at the Galdoni and gave a little shrug. He tipped his head with a smile of understanding.

I turned back. "We've gone through a few things together." Several laughs rose at the understatement. "It hasn't been easy." I rubbed my eyes in an attempt to keep my emotions at bay, but seeing all of the students looking at me, hanging onto my words, who had survived the Galdoni with me, was too much. "My start here was bumpy, to say the least." My voice cracked. "I may not have been a great people-person, and I don't think you knew what to do with me, either."

My shoulder ached where the knife had stabbed it. I rubbed it as I spoke. "But when Ava came here, I saw what integration really meant." I looked back at her. "She wasn't afraid, and so neither were you. She smiled, and you accepted her. She became my rock at this school, and you know what I saw?"

Tears broke free and trailed down my face. "When those gunmen came looking for Ava, you hid her without regard for your own safety. You were threatened at gunpoint, yet she was one of you, and you weren't about to give her up. You are far braver than I was. I knew I could fight them, maybe not stop them, but I grew up training to fight and not be afraid. You didn't grow up at gunpoint." A few students laughed, but there were tears in the eyes of many. They watched me without speaking, and their expressions gave me strength.

"I never thought our presence here would be a danger to you; it was never our intention to bring fear into your lives. Yet you have stood by us without shunning our differences. You allowed me to realize that it was me who had created the barrier between us, a barrier I am proud to say is gone." I smiled and cheers went up. I held out my hand and they quieted. "I have something to ask of you now. It may be dangerous, but our hope is to eliminate any danger to you. It is the chance we need to track down the threat to Ava and put an end to these attacks for good."

They listened to my plan with such charged silence I felt every word echo back at me from the walls of the gymnasium. When I finished, I handed the microphone to Principal Kelley. I took a seat next to Ava. She leaned against my good shoulder. I slipped my hand into hers, borrowing strength from her touch. The pain I had pushed to the back of my mind surfaced. I gritted my teeth and waited.

Not a sound followed. Principal Kelley watched the students carefully, worry clear on his face. "We're going to vote," he said. "The easiest way will be to vote by applause. Any who feel that Reece's plan is too dangerous, please show it by clapping now."

If anything, the silence in the room increased. I realized I was holding my breath, and I let it out slowly. Saro reached over and squeezed my shoulder. I gave him a small smile.

"Any who feel we should try Reece's plan. . . ." The applause that answered drowned out his next words. He looked back at me.

I nodded, feeling relief and as though a weight had been placed on my shoulders at the same time. I stood and Principal Kelley handed me the microphone again. The crowd quieted. "We must keep our plans quiet so whoever is behind the attacks won't find out. This may be our only shot. I appreciate your support more than I can say. You have become my brothers and sisters, and I will do everything in my power to keep you safe."

A roar answered my words. Students stomped in the bleachers and yelled; teachers instigated clapping and shouting. I met Mr. Bennett's gaze. He nodded in approval. Principal Kelley accepted the microphone back. Ava and I walked arm in arm off the platform. The instant we were on the ground, we were swarmed by students.

"I'm so excited to be a part of this!" Sam gushed.

"Do you think I should bring a gun?" a boy with spiked hair asked. Several of the students gave nervous laughs.

I shook my head. "No guns on school property. If all goes as planned, you won't need it."

"I'm going to wear purple," Alicia said. "Or maybe pink."

"Does that mean I have to rent a tuxedo?" a boy protested.

The group around us laughed.

"Do exactly what you would do for the prom," I told him.

He grinned, showing crooked teeth. "Overalls it is."

"Johnny," the blonde-haired girl at his side protested, slapping his shoulder.

I glanced over to see Randy talking with Ava. She laughed and set a hand on his arm. Jealousy surged through me. I turned back to the students with an effort. "I've got to go." I was surprised to see disappointment on many faces.

"You're skipping school?" Brian asked good-naturedly.

I nodded. "Doctor's orders. You know Dr. Ray's strict when all the Galdoni know not to go against what he says."

"How bad was it?" a kid I recognized from the party asked.

I glanced back at Kale and Saro. They were busy honing our plans with the principal. I lifted up my shirt. The stitches Dr. Ray had redone along my side could be seen through the light dressing. Gasps and a few exclamations could be heard. I pulled my shirt back down.

"How's your shoulder?" Seth asked.

I moved it experimentally, and hid a wince at the pain. "It took a few more of Dr. Ray's stitches. If I keep it up, I'll have more scars from outside the Academy than within."

Chuckles met my words. It felt good to joke about the Academy and the way things had gone at the school. The fact that we could laugh about it together made me feel like I was one of them. Alice threw her arms around my neck. "Thank you again. You were so brave."

Several of the other girls followed. I glanced over to see Kale and Saro watching me with wide grins on their faces. I backed out of the tight embraces. "Uh, you're welcome. You guys were the brave ones, coming to my rescue like that."

"I led the charge," Brian pointed out.

I held out a hand. "Thanks, man. The distraction saved my life."

He shook my hand and I smothered a cry at the pain that ran through my shoulder. "Anytime. You think we could get Coach to let you play football? You'd be unstoppable as a receiver."

I laughed at the thought. "There's probably a rule against flying on the field."

"And if there were any fights, the other team would be gonners," he said with a laugh.

The thought made me sober. I nodded and forced a smile. "I've got to go. Thank you, everyone."

I left them talking excitedly about the plans. Even though we were impinging on the prom, students were talking about dresses and flowers as if they didn't mind. I passed Ava and Randy on the way to the door.

"What do you say? Want to go to the prom with me?" Randy asked.

My blood ran cold. I ducked out the door into the sunlight. I leaned against the wall and let the golden warmth fall on my face and shoulders. It was a warm contrast to the chill inside me.

Ava was my girl.

I shook my head, correcting myself. She was nobody's girl. She could do whatever she pleased, and she deserved to be happy. Randy was a star on the football team, he fit in with her circle of friends, and the way she smiled at him made my stomach turn because it was close to the smile she gave me, not quite, but close. I wanted to beat him senseless. My hands clenched into fists.

I had to stop resorting to violence to resolve things. Even entertaining the thought of watching him cry was wrong, though I had to admit it brought a bit of joy to think about. I had to learn to control my anger. Ava deserved better.

I turned and leaned my forehead against the rough red bricks. The sun bathed my blue wings with heat. Ava didn't deserve an animal who couldn't control his rage. She needed someone she could trust, who had the normal life she wanted. I definitely didn't have a normal life.

"Are you okay?"

I turned at the concern in Saro's voice. The Galdoni's golden wings gleamed in the sunshine.

I nodded. "I'm fine."

His expression said he thought otherwise. "It's probably time we get you back."

I grimaced at the thought of the medical floor's white walls. "Any chance I could stay for class?"

Saro looked me up and down. "I don't want to point out the fact that you look like you're going to fall over, but you do look like you're going to fall over. Besides, I thought we all decided it was best if you and Ava didn't enter the school again until prom to keep it from becoming a target when we're not ready."

I nodded. "You're right. I think I'm just tired of waiting."

A smile hinted on his face. "We just came up with the plan."

I studied at the sidewalk. "I mean waiting for my life to begin, to find where I fit in and to make my own place in this world."

A shadow of concern crossed Saro's face. "I thought you had that here."

"I thought I did, too," I admitted quietly.

He fell silent. It was one of the things I really appreciated about the Galdoni. When he didn't have anything to say, he let silence speak. There were so many things I worked out about myself in the amiable silences we shared.

I was surprised when he broke the silence first. "You know no life is normal, right?"

"What do you mean?"

He nodded toward the gymnasium. "You would be wrong to think a human has a normal life. No two lives are the same in there."

"It's got to be more normal than what I have, living in a bare room on the floor of a building filled with killers who eat together and train together as if we weren't the product of a blood-thirsty society." I regretted the words as soon as I spoke them. I had made a point never to complain because the Galdoni Center was so much better than the Academy there really was no comparison. Now I couldn't take the words back.

Saro stood with his hands behind his back and his head bowed for a moment. With the sun behind him, he looked like a winged angel lit up in gold. My conversation with Koden came back to me and I remembered the picture of the angel with the lamb in its arms.

"It was your choice to live in a bare room," Saro reminded me gently without looking up. He rubbed his hands together slowly, studying the burn scars that ran along his skin. "And yes, Galdoni are killers, but we are also so much more. We live, we breathe, we dream, we hurt, and we love just like the humans here." He glanced at me. "If you put someone in a box, you will only be disappointed when they break free. No one, not even the Galdoni, deserve to be classified in a box any more than we deserved to be chained in cells."

Guilt pounded through me at his words. I knew them, and by his kind tone, I knew he knew that as well. He continued, "I'm grateful for this blood-thirsty society."

Surprised, I stared at him. "Why?"

He shrugged with a small smile. "Because first of all, we wouldn't be here without it; secondly, I feel that the humans' understanding toward violence is why we've been allowed to integrate into society. Since they created us, in a way, they understand us. We're more similar than both sides want to admit. That's why this will work out; deep down we know we're the same."

His words brought a small smile to my lips. I glanced back at the gymnasium. He was right. Brayce's need to control his life at school because he had no say over what had happened at home was one I could understand very well. When the Galdoni attacked, I saw students who protected each other at the risk of their own lives; that's what I had done. The opposite of violence was compassion, and I had seen that when Ava came to Crosby High. They took her in like she was one of them, and that compassion had spread to me through my actions. Ava was right to want a normal life here. It was a good place to begin.

Kale, Principal Kelley, and Ava came through the door. Ava smiled when she saw me and crossed to my side. She set her head on my shoulder. "I lost you in there."

"I think it was the opposite," I said before I could stop myself.

At her questioning look, I forced a smile and lifted my arm. She ducked under it and leaned against me.

"Looks like we have our work cut out for us until Saturday," Principal Kelley said. "We'll see you guys soon."

I lifted my wings. The movement pulled at my shoulder that was very sore from its second set of stitches. I gritted my teeth and pushed them down. The others rose into the air around me. I put a hand to the wound. Pressure against my shoulder eased the pain of working the muscles, but not by much.

"We could take a taxi," Kale said.

I threw him a smile. "And miss flying? Not a chance." I pushed my wings down harder. Ava laughed and kept up with me. It reminded me of the first time we had flown together. She had chased me into the clouds and told me about Superman. There were no clouds that morning, but the feeling of the sun was radiant as we broke above the buildings. I spread my wings out to soar; it put a lot less pressure on my shoulder to ride the wind.

"Let's fly to the ocean," I proposed.

Kale smiled. "You're avoiding the Center."

I shook my head. "I'm avoiding Dr. Ray. He didn't approve of our flight this morning."

Saro chuckled. "He was the one who recommended the taxi."

"Give the man some wings," I said. "Then we'll see who choses riding in a car."

I watched Ava fly. The feathers of her dark gray wings ruffled gently with the breeze. It caught her hair, making the long black locks flow over her shoulders like an ocean current. There was a look of pure enjoyment on her face as if she felt exactly the same way about flying that I did. Her hands opened, catching the wind and making it dance over her fingers. She glanced at me. A smile spread across her face, lighting her sea green eyes. It was the smile she saved only for me. Pain flared in my chest.

Chapter Sixteen

I tipped my wings toward the Center. The others followed. Kale and Saro landed on the roof. I dove toward the medical floor. I expected Ava to land on the eighth, but she followed me. The door buzzed on the print reader. Ava's footsteps echoed mine as I went to the small room filled with monitors and equipment. I grabbed my toothbrush and the clothes I had been wearing when the Galdoni attacked.

"What are you doing?" Ava asked in surprise.

"Going back to my room," I replied shortly.

"Didn't Dr. Ray want you here for a few more days? He said you needed monitoring in case you got an infection or the stitches pulled through."

I glanced at her. The concern on her face was more than I could take. I felt my control slipping. "I'm not a weakling, Ava. I can take care of myself. You do whatever you want. I'm not going to stop you."

I walked past her into the hallway. I had definitely pushed myself too far. The thought of flying up to the ninth floor felt like too much. I walked to the balcony anyway.

"What are you talking about?" Ava asked, following me. "What is going on, Reece?"

I forced my wings to open. The pain of the movement had intensified after the long flight. I put a hand against my shoulder, willing it to ease.

"Maybe we should take the elevator," Ava suggested, her voice filled with warm concern. "You're pale and I can tell you're hurting."

Anger that she thought I was weak flooded through me. With the pain and the loss of control I was feeling, I snapped. "I'm fine. You'd be better without me, Ava, and you know it."

I stepped off the balcony. It wasn't my smartest moment. My muscles had locked up and my right wing didn't want to respond at all. The left managed only to slow my fall and spin me enough so that it looked like I would smash into the Galdoni Center before plummeting to the ground. That would be a fine death; the honorable crashing into a building before plunging to a bone-breaking stop on the sidewalk. They didn't teach us that at the Academy.

A hand grabbed mine. I looked up to see the determination on Ava's face as she pushed her wings hard to slow my descent. We landed on the grass and I collapsed on my back. She joined me, her chest rising and falling as she fought to catch her breath from the exertion.

"That was stupid," I admitted when I could get my mind around the fact that I wasn't dead.

"Yes, it was," Ava replied. There was anger in her voice. She rose up on one elbow and demanded, "What were you thinking? That falling to your death would be fun?"

I held up a hand, but couldn't gather the strength to do more than that. "To be honest, I thought I could still fly."

She shook her head, her black hair sliding past her shoulder. "Why do you think I suggested the elevator? You looked like you were nearly dead already."

I cracked a smile. "I thought you suggested it out of spite. I'd rather die out here than in there."

She let out an angry huff at that and slapped my good shoulder. "Reece, you need to pull it together. I don't know what's wrong with you."

The worry in her tone ate at my stubborn pride. I wanted to fight, to hit something and put all of my anger into it, but at the moment I couldn't stand and so I had to settle for the truth. "I heard Randy ask you to the prom."

Ava fell silent. I glanced up at her, but she was silhouetted by the sun. I shielded the light from my eyes in an attempt to see her expression. When I did, my heart skipped a beat.

"You thought I would say yes," she said quietly. She touched my cheek, her hand gentle. Her eyebrows pulled together. "Why would I say yes?"

I forced myself up onto one elbow. "Because he's your key to a normal life, Ava."

A slight, sad smile touched her lips and she shook her head. "There are no normal lives, Reece."

"Have you been talking to Saro?" I asked.

"What?" She gave me a confused look.

"Never mind." I took a calming breath. "I just feel like I stand in the way of the simple life you want. With me, you'll always be reminded that you're different. You should go with Randy. Don't worry about me. You have my blessing."

I studied the grass under my hand. After a moment, I settled back so that I was laying on it once more with sunlight bathing my face. I closed my eyes. It would be easy for Ava to leave and save face. She didn't owe me anything. She was her own person.

"I told Randy no," she said.

There was a funny tone to her voice that made me open my eyes. I glanced up at her, forgetting about the sun. It was so bright it made my eyes water. I shielded them from the light. "What? Why?"

She gave me a little smile. "Because we have nothing in common. All he wants to talk about is football, and I was hoping somebody else would ask me even though he hasn't shown any indication of doing so."

I frowned at that. Another surge of jealous filled me so strong my hands clenched into fists. "Who? Brian?"

Ava laughed. The sound was so light it chased the anger from my chest like a balloon popped with a pin. She pushed my shoulder. "You, silly. I've been waiting for you to ask."

Realization flooded me. I covered my face with my hands. "I've been so stupid," I said.

She pulled my hands away. "Jumping off the balcony without being able to fly was stupid. Being jealous of me is, well, kind-of sweet." Her smile deepened. "Are you crying?"

I wiped my watery eyes. "It's the sun," I protested.

She laughed. "I know today's been hard on you. . . ."

"It's the sun," I replied again with a laugh. I pointed. "It's right over your head, so whenever I look at you, it about kills me!"

"Sure," she said with a teasing grin.

I let my head fall back. "I'm sorry, Ava."

She fell silent for a moment. When she spoke, her voice was gentle. "You still haven't asked me."

That brought a smile to my face. I reached up and pulled her to my side. She cuddled against my good shoulder. "Ava, my beautiful, sweet, angelic Ava, will you go to the prom with me?"

At her silence, I glanced down at her. She gave me another teasing smile. "Will it make you cry?" At my laughing protest, she sat up and looked down at me again, a warm smile on her face and the sunlight bright in her eyes. "I will go to the prom with you, Reece, on one condition."

Trepidation filled me. "What's that?"

She grinned. "You have to wear a tux."

That made me laugh. "I'm not sure any tuxedo place is going to be able to fit these." I tipped my head toward my wings.

"We'll find one," she promised. "It'll be an adventure." She helped me sit up slowly.

"I would have thought you'd had enough adventures with me," I told her.

She eased me carefully to my feet and ducked under my arm. "With you? Never."

I grinned as we made our way to the front doors and the elevator.

***

"Are you sure they're going to be cool with this?" I asked, looking up doubtfully at the store labeled Fancy Pants.

"Don't worry," Mrs. Brunsky reassured me. "I called ahead just to be sure." She led the way into the store.

Getting tuxedos and dresses for the prom had turned into a social event. Apparently everyone thought it would be fun to dress up the Galdoni. While I detested the idea, the excitement on Ava's face was enough to drag me anywhere. Kale's reassurance before we left that he had placed a card on file at the store filled all the girls with dangerous enthusiasm.

"Can't we wear jeans?" Brian asked for the twentieth time. Alice dragged him through the door. He gave me a look of sheer agony before he disappeared behind the glass.

"I'll iron my dad's church pants," Seth protested. "He's a bit taller than me, but they should look alright if I roll them up at the ankles."

Sam shook her head. "We're not going for *alright*. We're going for fabulous." He followed her inside with his head hanging like a scolded dog.

"Sounds like I'm not the only one reluctant to be fitted like a doll," I told Ava.

She laughed. "Come on. It'll be fun!"

I let her lead me inside.

Fancy Pants was split into two halves, the right side filled to the brim with dresses in every color imaginable, and the left stocked with straight rows of pants, vests, shirts, ties, cummerbunds, and anything else torturous individuals had invented to make women look beautiful and men look like penguins. There were even top hats in one corner.

Alice grabbed Ava's arm. "Let's go!" she said, giddy with excitement. "Mom's already found the scarlet dresses."

Ava gave me an apologetic look. "I didn't know we'd be splitting up."

I gave a self-suffering sigh. "Go ahead. I think I can manage."

"You sure?"

I couldn't help but nod at the bright smile on her face. "Definitely. Go have fun."

She squeezed my hand and skipped off with Alice.

"We've been expecting you."

It was all I could do to keep from chopping the man in the throat followed by a punch to the stomach and then an elbow in the back to lay him groaning on the floor. He must have seen the look on my face when I turned, because he backed off a few steps.

"Haven't you heard not to sneak up on a Galdoni?" I asked, willing my heartbeat to slow.

He held up his hands. "Sorry, sorry. A bad habit. Makes for good sells when I see someone looking at things a bit higher priced; I tend to notice everything." He wrung his hands together with an apologetic smile. "I noticed you could have killed me just then."

I let out a slow breath. "I try not to kill people," I said dryly. "But you might have been in pain for the next week or so."

The man gave a weak smile. "Thank you for your constraint."

I nodded.

"I'm Stewart," he introduced himself.

"Reece," I replied.

His smile deepened and I followed his gaze to my wings. "Wow. I could find you a vest to match them. It would look fabulous with that color of blue. And it would set off your blue eyes so magnificently. You would be the belle of the ball!"

I shook my head quickly. "Uh, no thanks. No belle. I'd prefer to draw as little attention as possible."

Stewart gave a short little laugh. "As if," he replied. "I'll bet you're the center of attention wherever you go." At my disgruntled look, he pursed his lips. "Alright; little attention. Point taken. What did you plan to wear, if I may be so bold as to ask?"

I looked at Seth and Brian thumbing through the vests. There was every color imaginable. An idea occurred to me. "You see that Galdoni over there?" I tipped my head toward Ava who was busy holding the dozen dresses Alice had already handed her.

Stewart followed my gaze. Something in his face softened when he spotted her. I had seen the same thing every time someone new looked at Ava. It affirmed how special she was, how different. Nobody could help but smile when they looked at her. "She's gorgeous," Stewart breathed.

I nodded. "Do you have a vest that matches the color of her wings?"

Stewart's mouth fell open. He covered it with a hand, but it remained open. "That is the most romantic thing. . . ." He paused, at a loss for words. His mouth gaped a moment more, then he shut it and stepped to attention so that his heels actually clicked together. "Your wish is mine to fulfill. Follow me."

Surprised by his suddenly commanding air, I trailed him through the rows of clothes to a rack of vests near Seth. He held up a green and yellow one. "What do you think?"

I tried not to smile at the dismay Sam would show if he wore it. "I think you should go with something a little less bold."

"Less bold, right," Seth mumbled. He thumbed through the rack. "How about this one?" He held up a brown and orange vest.

I didn't know what to say, but when Stewart turned around and saw what Seth was holding, he dropped everything in his arms. "Goodness sakes, son. You can't wear that with your red hair!" He nudged me with his elbow. "Who'd be the center of attention now?"

"Maybe we should let him wear it," I suggested.

Stewart laughed so loud it caught us both by surprise. He leaned on my shoulder as he laughed and laughed. Seth and I exchanged a look of disbelief. "It wasn't that funny," I said under Stewart's laughter.

Seth grinned. "Apparently, he thinks you're hilarious."

When Stewart was finally sane once again, he ran two fingers over his eyebrows before picking up the vests he had dropped. "Come with me," he told Seth.

Seth gave me a look of helpless panic. Stewart snapped and he hurried over to accept the armful of vests the man held out. "Try these on. One will hopefully suit your fancy." Stewart winked at me. "Get it? Suit your fancy? And this is a suit store?"

I cracked a smile and it set him off laughing again. Bewildered, I followed him to a rack of gray and silver vests.

"Okay, okay," he said, wiping his eyes. "You've got to let me work. I can't imagine I'd get anything done if you were here cracking jokes all day." He pointed at the vests. "Are her wings more of a light gray like this?"

I shook my head. "No, they're dark like storm clouds, but they lighten at the edges, like—"

"The sun breaking through and casting the entire day in glorious light?" Stewart finished helpfully.

"I, uh, yeah," I replied, at a loss for words. I ran a finger along the rack, feeling the soft silk. When I neared the darker grays, one stood out. "This one. This is the color."

"Ah," Stewart breathed. "Spectacular. I'm sure our tailor can make this work with your wings. We just need to find a suit with the proper fit." He pulled out a tape measure and began talking numbers faster than I could follow. "Hmm, yes," he mumbled. "Wide shoulders, but I suppose that would be expected with the extra flight muscles." More measurements. "Do you work out?" he asked.

"A bit," I replied, unsure where he was going with the question. "But I'm not allowed to train."

"Of course, of course," he mumbled, back in his cadence. "I could just tell with all the muscles. . . ."

I blocked him out and turned my attention to the girls. Ava had so many dresses in her arms I could barely see her. Emily threw a green one on top, then picked up her own pile. All of the girls followed Alice and Sam into the dressing rooms. Mrs. Brunsky waited outside with her hands clasped in anticipation.

At first when Alice insisted that Ava and I go along, Mrs. Brunsky had been concerned about having two Galdoni in her vehicle. Fortunately, all she had to do was meet Ava for her worries to be alleviated. It had been determined by Alice that there wasn't a clothing store with appropriate prom wear for everyone, so our trip took us to the nearby city of Tremonton. By the time we reached the store, Mrs. Brunsky seemed perfectly happy to have us along. She now beamed at Ava as if the Galdoni was her own daughter.

"If you would step into the fitting room," Stewart said.

When I looked at him, I realized by his expression that he had probably repeated the request several times.

"Sorry," I replied. "I was a bit, um. . . ."

"Distracted?" he completed helpfully. At my nod, he smiled. "You wouldn't be the first gentleman whose attentions were captured by a beautiful lady across the way. It is one of the allures of our fine establishment."

I followed him to the dressing room door and accepted the items he handed me. "Now keep in mind that these are unfitted, and you give us an additional challenge in accommodating your wings. Your group hasn't given us much notice, but I feel we'll be able to have proper attire available by Saturday if we ensure that our measurements are precise." He held up his tape measure.

I sighed and stepped into the room.

Chapter Seventeen

"Look who's fancy now," Seth exclaimed when I walked out of the elevator. He and Sam stood arm in arm next to Alice and Brian.

"Looking sharp, Reece," Bear called from the front desk.

"Thank you, Bear," I replied. "Maybe dressing up isn't all that bad."

"That's what I say," Bear agreed. He smoothed the front of the printed tuxedo tee-shirt he had chosen to wear in celebration of the fact that Ava and I were going to prom.

His grin was contagious. I felt it spread across my face without effort.

"I got you this to give to Ava," Seth said. He handed me a clear box with a flower inside. "It goes around her wrist." He grinned. "Sam's mom informed me that it is a very important part of going to prom, even though it's just a flower."

Sam laughed, patting Seth's arm. "It's called a corsage," she explained. "And every girl who goes to prom deserves one." She held up her wrist to show off the blue and purple flowers that matched her dress.

"Thank you for helping me out," I told her.

She gave me a warm smile. "It's no secret that this is your first prom. Well, it's ours, too, but we've of course heard about it forever and I wouldn't want you to mess it up for Ava even though you are already doing an exceptional job. I can't believe you actually matched her wings, and after all you've been through, you're still taking her even though you're pale and probably—"

Alice put a hand on her shoulder. "Sam, you're babbling."

Sam covered her mouth. "I am," she said with a giggle from behind her hand.

Seth grinned at her. "It's alright. I enjoy Sam's babbling."

The fond look she gave him turned his cheeks as red as his hair.

The elevator behind me beeped. I glanced over my shoulder.

It would have been cheesy to say I felt like I could fly, because I could fly, but the moment Ava stepped out of the elevator I forgot I had feet, hands, or wings, because the world stood still. I felt like I floated straight to her side.

"You look absolutely gorgeous," I said when I found my voice.

She had chosen a deep blue dress that accentuated her curves and trailed to the floor. The graceful lines and empire cut waist matched the fall of her feathers. She smiled at my vest. "You matched my wings."

I nodded, but before I could say anything, Alice called from across the room, "And she matched your wings! It's so romantic." I glanced back to see her slap the shoulder of Brian's red vest. "And you said we had to wear school colors. I hate yellow!"

I held up the corsage. "This is for you."

Ava's smile tugged at my heart. I fumbled with the box, but couldn't get it open. She held out a hand. "May I?" In two seconds, she had the box open and was holding the corsage. "It's so beautiful!" she exclaimed.

I slid it on her wrist and smiled at Seth over her head. He gave me a thumb's up. "You're welcome," Sam called with a giddy smile.

I held out my arm. "My lady."

"Oh," Ava said with a little laugh. "Why, thank you." She rested her hand on the crook of my elbow and we walked to the others.

"You should go everywhere dressed like that," Alice said. "You two look absolutely amazing."

"You look beautiful," Ava replied. "You definitely should wear yellow more often."

Alice beamed at Brian. "See, I told you we should wear school colors," she said.

Seth led the way through the door. He was proud of his newly attained driver's license and his father had lent him their family's van.

"I don't know how I'm supposed to explain riding to prom in a van," Alice said. She picked a toy soldier off the back seat and examined it between two fingers before tossing it to the floor.

I refrained from mentioning that Kale had offered to pay for a limousine. Seth had been so excited at the prospect of driving everyone that I couldn't take it away from him. Ava and I squished on the middle row of seats. It was a bit difficult with our wings, but we made it work.

Ava leaned her head on my shoulder. "I'm nervous," she whispered in my ear.

"It's going to be fine," I whispered back. "I promise." She squeezed my fingers. I rubbed my thumb soothingly along the top of her hand. I glanced back at Alice and Brian, then met Seth's gaze in the rearview mirror. "Everyone remember the drill?" They all nodded. Though excitement lay heavy in the air, Ava's worry showed on everyone's faces. "It's going to be okay," I reassured them. "Just breathe, stay calm, and remember what we practiced."

"They're Galdoni," Alice said, her voice tight.

I nodded. "I promise I won't let anything happen to any of you, and I have help this time."

"Thank goodness," Brian exclaimed from behind me. He squeezed my good shoulder. "Because I don't know how many more times you can take a beating."

"As many as it takes," I reassured him. "But our hope is no violence. It's going to be a walk in the park." I looked out the window and let out a slow breath, willing myself to believe my words.

When we reached the gymnasium, students were pouring out of vehicles and admiring each other's attire.

"You all look so beautiful!" Alice exclaimed. "Emily! Alicia!" she grabbed Ava's hand. "Be right back, Reece." They took off across the sidewalk.

I tried to keep the worry from my face as I watched Ava. I could feel eyes watching us. Seth and Sam were busy conversing with Mr. Bennett who manned the front door. Even he had seen fit to dress up for the night.

"Nice tux," I told him when I reached the door.

"Thank you," he replied. "Same to you. I didn't know they made tuxedos for Galdoni."

I smiled. "We found a tailor who was kind enough to take the time for alterations."

"Paid him a lot?" Mr. Bennett guessed.

"He probably made half a year's salary off us," I replied.

My algebra teacher laughed. "Only a tailor would rip off a Galdoni."

I shrugged. "He knows I won't be back there anytime soon."

Mr. Bennett's grin faltered. "Is everything good?" He tipped his head slightly to indicate the students.

I nodded. "Let's get everyone inside. The sooner, the better."

He raised his voice. "The dance is about to begin."

Smiles faded slightly and eyes shifted as if the students suddenly remembered why they were there. Everyone greeted Mr. Bennett as normally as possible and shuffled through the door. I waited for Ava.

"They're all nervous," she whispered.

"I am, too," I admitted.

She took a calming breath. "You've got this," she said.

Her confidence filled me with strength. I brought her close and kissed her while I had the chance. A few catcalls and laughs followed. I smiled down at her. "No matter what happens, I love you."

"I love you, too, Reece," she said, looking up at me with her sea green eyes that made me forget what I was doing.

"Ahem," Mr. Bennett said. "Not to take any attention away from you, but there's a dance to attend to," he reminded me.

I grinned, feeling more like myself. "Thank you, Mr. Bennett. Why don't you head in first?" I held the door open.

He hesitated, then nodded. "Good luck," he said under his breath when he passed.

Ava took my arm and we stepped through the door. Inside, the gymnasium had been transformed into a ballroom. The prom committee had chosen red and gold as the colors. Streamers, balloons, and paper flowers hung everywhere, but there wasn't time to enjoy it.

Galdoni from the Center guided Mr. Bennett along with the students up the stairs to the balcony that surrounded the top level of bleachers. The students waited silently behind the bleachers where they wouldn't be seen. Galdoni with long trench coats to hide their wings lined the floor. A few of the female Galdoni who had volunteered wore dresses with Velcro backs and lots of layers to hide any questionable lumps. Ava and I walked onto the gymnasium floor and Galdoni couples followed, acting the parts they had practiced.

A song started. I let out a slow breath and began the waltz steps all the students had been taught in prom rehearsal. Ava danced so gracefully I felt like an oaf compared to her. She was the embodiment of beauty. I found myself watching her with the hope that the moment would go on forever. I almost forgot why we were there surrounded by fake couples dressed like humans, and why the students and teachers were hiding behind the bleachers on the upper level.

The door to the gymnasium flew open, reminding me without a doubt. Ava and I slowed our dance.

"Stay calm," I whispered. "It'll be alright."

"Give us the girl," a Galdoni with hulking gray wings demanded.

Ava and I backed away toward the far corner like we had planned. There were six Galdoni this time. Apparently going up by twos with every attack seemed like a good strategy to someone.

"Give us the girl and no one gets hurt," the Galdoni repeated, pursuing us across the gymnasium floor with the other Galdoni right behind.

"Good," Kale said into my earpiece. "Keep them moving."

When we reached the corner, I positioned Ava behind me. "Touch her and I'll break your neck," I said.

"Do you have to antagonize them?" Kale asked exasperatedly in my ear.

The leader stepped closer. "I'd like to see you try, kid." He glanced at my wings and his eyes narrowed. "You're the one who broke Steel's arm."

"He had it coming," I replied.

"Reece," Kale warned in the earpiece.

"He said he was outnumbered," the Galdoni argued.

I shrugged. "Or it could be because he chose a stupid name like Steel."

The leader's eyes narrowed. "He happens to be my friend."

I lifted an eyebrow. "Perhaps your friends need to learn not to mess with me. Their limbs might stay intact longer."

The Galdoni's hands clenched into fists. His weight shifted onto his front foot. He was about to lunge. My muscles tensed in response.

The door to the gymnasium slammed open once more. All the Galdoni looked back in time to see Officer Donaldson lead his team into the room. The Galdoni in disguise around us threw off their coats.

The leader glared at me. A vein bulged in his neck as he fought to remain calm. "You set us up," he said in a dangerous growl.

I took the earpiece out in a casual gesture to hide how tense my muscles were at his proximity to Ava. "We set a trap and you were kind to oblige," I answered.

A roar tore from him and he attacked with fists swinging. I ducked under the first swing as a tranquilizer dart hit him in the back. I slugged him in the left kidney, then spun back and elbowed him in the jaw. Unfortunately, with the wounds in my shoulder, there wasn't as much strength behind the elbow as there should have been.

He grabbed me in a bear hug as he fell backwards from the effects off the tranquilizer dart. The motion sent pain tearing through my side. I turned so that my weight rested behind the same elbow. It drove into his stomach when we hit the floor. I rolled to the left and came up in a crouch, ready to take him out. His head lolled to the side.

"Easy tiger," Officer Donaldson said. He stood a few steps away, his tranquilizer gun pointed at the fallen Galdoni. "He's out."

I nodded, but kept my attention on him in case he wasn't as unconscious as he looked. Officer Donaldson put handcuffs on him. I rubbed my shoulder and glanced around the room. The rest of the attacking Galdoni were being handcuffed and led out the door. There were a few protests, but they were sorely outnumbered. Nobody wanted to be shot with a tranquilizer like their leader.

"That worked out better than I could have hoped," Officer Donaldson said. He motioned for his men to drag the Galdoni away. "Good work, Reece."

Ava hurried to my side. "Are you alright?" she asked, concern thick in her voice.

I nodded with a relieved smile. "Just fine." She threw her arms around me in a tight hug.

Kale and Saro came out of the crowd who led the Galdoni away. "Good plan," Kale said. "Though you probably could have watched what you said a bit more carefully."

I handed the earpiece back to him. "Then they would have known it was a trap."

Saro laughed. "That's what I told him." He smiled at Ava. "Kale's always giving me a hard time for my mouth, but it's gotten me out of more than one bad situation."

"And into quite a few more," Kale concluded.

Saro grinned and nodded toward Officer Donaldson's gun. "You found stronger tranquilizers."

The police officer smiled. "I told you I'd keep searching. These are experimental, but they seem to do the job."

Principal Kelley appeared at the top of the second level. "Is it over?"

"We're done here," Officer Donaldson called up. "We'll clear the area and your students are free to begin their prom."

Cheers and the sound of footsteps answered his words as students hurriedly left their shelter behind the bleachers and ran for the windows to see the arrested Galdoni be loaded into the waiting police vehicles. The DJ started a pop song. A smile spread across Kale's face. "You guys have fun."

"You could always stay," I suggested. "You've never been to a school dance."

"Wouldn't that be like having your father at the prom?" Kale asked.

Ave and I laughed. "You're three years older than me," I pointed out. "You would have graduated a year ago, and Saro would be graduating this year if you were students."

"Exactly," Kale said with a nod. "We're too old for this stuff."

"Yeah," Saro concluded, grinning at us both. "We'll leave it for the youngsters to enjoy. Besides, Skylar and Brie are waiting for us back at the Center. We promised them a date."

"Thanks for trusting me," I told them both.

"If you graduate with top grades, we may be able to get the police academy to reconsider their denial of Galdoni," Officer Donaldson said. He smiled at Saro. "I doubt they'd deny you a second time given all you've done since your first submission."

Saro returned the smile with a glimmer of hope in his eyes. "Let's see where this integration program takes us. Give it time."

"Deal," Officer Donaldson agreed.

***

Students were taking their places on the dance floor. Ava and I joined them. I watched Kale and Saro shake hands with Officer Donaldson and Principal Kelley before they left. Warmth flooded through me. The night had gone well. Everyone was safe, and we finally had a lead on Ava's attackers.

"You look extremely pleased with yourself," Ava said. She leaned against my chest. "As you should be."

"You did a good job pretending like you were terrified," I replied.

She looked up at me. "I was terrified."

I cupped her cheek in my hand. She smiled and tipped her head into my touch and closed her eyes. "I would never let anything happen to you," I said softly.

"I know," she replied. She opened her eyes and looked up at me again. "But I never want to be at someone's mercy again. They were too close. It scared me."

I nodded and wrapped my arms around her to help her feel safe. She ducked her head under my chin, her arms pulling me closer. I realized she was trembling. I hated that she was so afraid. I searched for a way to soothe her. "What if I teach you to fight?" I whispered into her hair. "What if you could defend yourself if something unexpected happens?"

She looked up at me in surprise. "You would do that?"

"Of course," I replied, smiling down at her. "Fear comes from the unknown. If you know you can defend yourself, you won't be so afraid."

She smiled, looking relieved. "I like that idea." We danced for several minutes before she looked up at me again. "Were you afraid?"

I grinned. "Terrified, but only because I was worried about you." I shrugged self-consciously. "I ran my mouth to keep his attention on me. I didn't want him to try anything."

She hugged me tight. "It worked, Reece. They'll get to the bottom of this because of your plan. You protected me just like you promised."

I hugged her back and whispered in her ear, "I'll always protect you, Ava."

We eventually took a seat at one of the decorated tables around the room. I eased down onto a chair, grateful for the rest. Seth and Sam joined us.

"What a night!" Sam exclaimed. "That was amazing!"

Seth nodded. "I can't believe you took that Galdoni down."

"It was the tranquilizer," I pointed out. "I really had nothing to do with it."

"Yeah," he pressed. "But you were ready to pulverize him. I saw it in your eyes. If he so much as looked at Ava, he was dead."

Ava's hand slipped into mine. I smiled at her. "I promised Ava nobody would hurt her."

Seth reached across the table and patted my shoulder. "Nobody will hurt you while I'm around."

My eyebrows rose. "Where were you during all of that?"

"Cowering, like the rest of the students," he admitted off-handedly. "But if my job wasn't to cower, I would have been there." He paused, then concluded, "I was a very good cowerer. Very convincing."

"Me, too," Sam said with a little laugh. "You should have seen us. Seth even tried to steal a kiss, telling me it was the last time we might ever have the chance before the Galdoni killed us all."

"Comforting," I mumbled. I glanced at Seth. "Did it work?"

He grinned. "She said I could kiss her anytime; I didn't have to wait for a death-threat by Galdoni attackers to do so." As if he had just realized what he said, he leaned over and kissed her. Sam kissed him back passionately.

Ava and I glanced at each other. Her smile matched mine, though I doubted the red blush across her cheeks looked the same on me.

"Want another dance?" I asked.

Her smile deepened. "Let's dance the night away."

Chapter Eighteen

"Learning to fight efficiently is all about using the most force while exerting the least amount of effort. You conserve your energy and can last much longer that way," I instructed. "Show me a fist."

Ava clenched her hands. She looked so cute in training pants that were far too big on her and a red tee-shirt with a bluebird on the front. It was her favorite shirt.

I checked her fist. "A bit looser. You don't want all your strength to go into your fist. More natural. That's right." I picked up on one of the training gloves that had a practice pad on the front. "Okay, now hit it."

"I don't want to hurt you," Ava protested.

I grinned at the thought. "You won't. It's padded. You can hit it as hard as you want."

"Alright," she said uncertainly. She pulled her fist back and hit the middle of the pad with the strength required to swat a fly.

"What was that?" I asked. "Where's all your ferocious energy?"

She laughed. "Ferocious, huh?" She punched the pad with more strength.

"Better," I nodded. "Much better." I pointed to the hanging bag. "Let's work on the bag. It'll help you direct your punch where you want it to land, and also see the results of your force. You can channel it better that way."

Ava punched the bag. Its chain rattled a bit. She gave me a pleased smile.

I nodded. "Nice. Now, turn with the punch, rotate so that all of your momentum is propelled to your contact point. It should start at your back foot so that when you turn, all of your strength is channeled into one smooth motion, like this." My right foot pivoted as I turned, shooting my arm out with the force of the rotation. The bag jumped on its chain and swung. I caught it on its way back to us.

"My turn," Ava said excitedly. She turned into the punch and managed to get the bag to swing slightly. She jumped up and down. "I got this!"

"You're a regular killing machine," I replied, laughing at her enthusiasm.

"How about kicks?" she asked. "You always throw in kicks when they're least expected."

I smiled. "I didn't know you were paying so much attention."

"I always pay attention to you," she replied. At my surprised look, she ducked her head. "That was cheesy." She looked up at me through lowered eyelashes.

The look banished my self-control. I pulled her close and kissed her. She let out a squeak of surprise, then returned my kiss, wrapping her arms gently around my shoulders. I stepped back with a sigh. "I think we just violated every principle of this room."

She laughed. "Kissing, fighting, it's the same, right?"

I put a hand to my racing heart. "Feels the same."

She smiled up at me with such love I could barely remember why we were there. I wanted to kiss her again, to hold her close and feel her pressed against me. I cleared my throat. "Well, uh, we'd better focus on those kicks."

I kicked the bag so hard it swung to the ceiling before coming back down. The pain that tore through my wounded side at the movement made me gasp. I was barely able to catch the bag before it bowled me over.

"That's my cue to sit this one out."

"Did you rip your stitches?" Ava asked worriedly as I eased down by the wall. "Dr. Ray said he would put you in a body cast."

I chuckled. "I know. It's the only way he thinks he can get me to hold still."

"I'm starting to agree with him," Ava said with her hands on her hips. She gave me a sweet, worried frown. "I don't know what to do with you, Reece."

"Keep smiling like that," I told her. "I don't feel a thing."

She laughed and hit my good shoulder. "I'm supposed to be the one training. You tell me what to do, and I'll do it." At my raised eyebrows, she grinned. "In training, Reece. Focus."

I reluctantly turned my attention back to her training regimen. There was so much to teach her, it was hard to figure out where to start, especially since I had begun my training at age three. "Try the kick," I instructed. My plan was to help her get the basics down, and then recruit Lem who had turned into a far better teacher than I ever could have hoped. Between the two of us, Ava would get the best training she could ask for.

***

That night, I couldn't sleep. I was about to give up and head to the roof when a slight tapping sounded on the floor. A smile spread across my face. With Ava's room directly beneath mine, we had come up with a tapping system for communicating. Four taps meant do you want company. I crouched on the floor and pounded two taps back with my knuckles. The carpet was thick so I had to hit a little harder, but the three taps that quickly responded made me smile. A few minutes later, her shadow was at the door. I turned on the lamp.

"What is this?" she exclaimed softly.

The fact that I actually had a lamp was a big step, but it was the rest of the room she talked about.

"Brie and Skylar helped me. I told them I was tired of living in a cell."

Ava's smile said more than words as she looked around the room. She studied the scenery pictures on the walls, one of a sunrise over a beautiful lake, the dock lit by the early morning glow as if welcoming the viewer to take a stroll, and the other of the sun rising behind a beautiful delicate red arch with sandstone all around. Brie said they spoke of new beginnings.

Ava's hand trailed along the blue cloth couch complete with soft gray pillows that matched her wings. She smiled at the fact that there were curtains hanging to the sides of the window. "It's wonderful, Reece." She paused at the sight of the picture frame by the lamp. She picked it up. "Where did you get this?"

I smiled at her hushed tone. "I bribed Koden to sneak around with a camera. Turns out he's a fair hand at photography."

196

"What did you bribe him with?" Ava asked, studying the picture.

"Wood for whittling. I cut some branches from a tree by the back doors. Don't tell anyone," I replied, watching her.

Ava's eyebrows were pulled together, her expression as if she didn't know whether to smile or cry. I held up my hand and she handed me the frame before sitting next to me on the bed.

"I didn't know if you would wake up," she said softly.

I nodded, a lump in my throat. Koden had taken the picture after we made it home from the party and I collapsed on the medical level. Dr. Ray did the best he could, but the days I slept, the doctor said Ava refused to leave the floor. The picture was of her staring into the window, one hand on the glass and a look of such worry on her face it ate at my heart every time I looked at it.

"It reminds me that someone cares," I told her quietly. "It's the first thing I see when I wake up in the morning and the last thing before I go to bed. I feel like I'm a better person because of it." I met her gaze. "Because if someone cares about you that much, you've got to be the best you can to deserve it."

She leaned over and kissed me. I closed my eyes and wrapped her in my arms. "I love you, Ava."

"I love you, Reece," she replied.

"There's more," I said, forcing myself to break away. I bent over gingerly. The action pulled at my stitches, but I didn't let the pain show. I pulled a book from beneath the bed. "Here."

"What's this?" she asked. She opened it and fell silent. Picture after picture lined the pages, and all of them were of her. In one, she was watching the sunset from the balcony. In another, she was eating in the cafeteria with Skylar, Brie, and

Alana. All four of the girls were laughing while Jayce, Alana's boyfriend, lay across the table holding a tray on his chest.

"This one's my favorite," I told her. I took the book and flipped to the last page. It was a picture of us lying on the grass as we had the day I fell from the balcony and she saved me. Her head was resting on my shoulder, my blue wings spread beneath us. It was beautiful in its simplicity, and also because of what it represented. "You saved my life that day."

"You saved mine many times," she said, her voice somewhat steady.

I shook my head. "When I saw you with Randy, I questioned everything, the point of this place, me going to school, even my existence. I felt like you deserved so much more, but that without you, I was nothing." I pointed at the picture. "That was the moment I realized with you in my arms, I had everything in the world."

She gave me such a sweet smile I had to answer it with a kiss. I smiled against her lips, my world complete.

Chapter Nineteen

"What are these?" Ava asked, thumbing through the pile by my lamp.

I glanced at them as I attempted to tie my shoes. "Bear brought those up. They're thank you cards from parents and students about the Galdoni thing."

Ava gave me an incredulous look. "And by *Galdoni thing*, you're referring to you jumping through the window and putting your life in danger to prevent students getting shot?"

I shrugged. "And the thing at Alice's party. It really doesn't matter."

"Doesn't matter?" Ava held up the stack. "There's like twenty letters here."

I pulled open the drawer below the lamp to reveal about four times that many. "The ones you're holding are the letters he brought up yesterday. Bear recommended they write because I don't have a phone," I explained, hoping to put off what I knew was coming.

"Reece, you've got to read these," Ava protested. "The people who wrote them are grateful for your sacrifice. You deserve to hear what they have to say."

I shook my head and pointed out, "Without us, they wouldn't have been in danger."

Ava speared me with a look. "So are you saying that if I wasn't in the audience and if someone came to the school only to shoot students and that Galdoni had nothing to do with it, you wouldn't have dived through that window?"

"Of course I would have," I replied.

She held up a hand before I could argue further. "Point for me. Now be quiet and take what you deserve."

I sat back on the bed with a long-suffering sigh.

She opened the first card. "Dear Mr. Galdoni." She looked up at me. "How formal." She cleared her throat. "Thank you for jumping on the bad guy." Her words slowed. "Because of you, my brother was able to come home." She held up the card; there was a picture drawn in crayon of a little boy in red standing next to his brother in blue. Ava blinked. "That may be the sweetest thing I've ever read."

She handed me the card. I looked at the child's penmanship and traced a finger along the drawing. She began the next one, which turned out to be a letter.

"Dear Reece, you don't know me, but I sit two seats up from you in our English class. At home, it's just my mom and I. My dad left us when I was ten, so I'm all my mom has left. So you see, if I don't come home, my mom has no one." Ava's brow creased as she continued, "I was sitting on the front row when the man with the gun and the Galdoni came in. I usually don't sit on the front row, and I don't know why I did that day. Jeff usually saves me a seat in the back with him, but he was home sick and those were the only seats left for the pep rally."

"There are splotches on the paper," Ava said quietly, interrupting her reading. "I think he was crying when he wrote this."

I set down the card and leaned forward with my elbows on my knees. The position hurt my side, but I didn't care. I closed my eyes and listened to the letter.

"When they came in, the man pointed the gun directly at me. I literally stared down the barrel, like they say in the old Westerns. And they're right. When you look at death, everything in your life flashes before your eyes. I'm not ready to die. My mom needs me, and someday if my dad ever comes back, I think he might need me, too. The man was yelling and swearing, but I didn't hear any of it. All I could hear was my heart pounding. I kept hoping that by the end of the day, it would still be pounding."

"Oh, Reece," Ava said in a heartbroken voice.

"I know," I replied softly.

She took a calming breath and continued, "When the glass broke with you diving through it, I thought it was the gun and I closed my eyes because I didn't want to watch myself die. When I opened them again, you had pulverized the man with the gun. The man was down, and the gun slid to a stop at my feet. I heard you fight the Galdoni, but I couldn't take my eyes off that gun. Because of you, the bullet didn't kill me. Because of you, I was able to go home to Mom and eat our favorite food, spaghetti, and talk about how crazy the day was. Because of you, I am alive to write this letter. Because of you, my whole life will go on as long as I don't do something stupid like step onto a road without looking and get hit by a car, which I won't do because I know what I would be missing now. Thank you for my life."

"It's signed by Trae Evans," Ava concluded quietly.

I sat in silence for a few minutes. I knew Trae. He was a good student. Mrs. Taylor called on him often in class and he always had an answer. I hadn't seen him at the assembly, but I knew where the gun stopped. I had glimpsed a pair of gray tennis shoes in front of it when I glanced over to be sure it was out of the fight before I was attacked by the Galdoni. I held out a hand and Ava gave me the letter.

She picked up the next one, some sort of card in a brown envelope. I was busy reading through Trae's letter again when Ava screamed.

"No!" she cried over and over again. "No, no, no, no!"

"What is it?" I asked, my heart pounding.

She held out the card. Two pictures fell to the ground. My heart stopped entirely at the sight of Seth and Sam tied up and bound to chairs. I used my foot to move it off the other picture, revealing Alice and Brian as well. Alice was crying and there was so much fear in her eyes I could barely breathe.

My fingers trembled as I held up the note. It was scrawled in rough penmanship.

"We have your friends. Call us so we can work out a trade. If cops or Galdoni show up other than you two, your friends will be killed without question." There was a number written on the bottom.

"We've got to go," Ava said, her voice on the edge of hysteria. "We've got to save them."

"Ava, wait!" I grabbed her arm. "We need help."

"You heard what the letter said. If we bring help, they die." She shook my hand off. "Reece, we have to go! Now! I'm not letting our friends suffer because of me."

I couldn't argue. She ran out the door and I hurried after her. I paused in the hallway. "We need a phone." I glanced into Saro's room. He wasn't there, but his cellphone was lying on the desk. I grabbed it and ran toward the balcony after Ava.

She walked from me to the balcony and back as I pressed the numbers with shaking fingers. A gruff voice answered. "About time. I thought you liked your friends too much to make them wait." I recognized the voice. It was Steel, the black-winged Galdoni from the attack at Alice's house.

"Your letter was mixed with a bunch of others. I wouldn't have even found it if it wasn't for Ava. How dare—"

The voice on the other end of the phone gave a dangerous chuckle. "How dare I?" Steel asked, his tone amused. "I dare because I have something you want, which is also a coincidence because you happen to have something I need very badly."

"You're not—"

"Meet us on the Parkway building in fifteen minutes. If you bring anyone, your friends die." The voice cut out.

I glared at the phone.

"What did he say?" Ava asked.

"They want to meet us on the Parkway building."

"Then let's go." She turned to the balcony.

I grabbed her hand. "Ava, it's risky. They want you for our friends. I'm not willing to make that trade."

Ava's eyes filled with tears. "It's me they want," she said passionately. "We'll find a way to fight them, but our friends aren't going to suffer for it. Who knows what they'll do if we don't show up? We need to buy us some time, and standing here isn't going to help."

"We need to tell Kale," I protested.

Ava shook her head. "I will not risk our friends getting a bullet because we disobeyed their orders. I'm going with or without you."

I had no choice. I shoved the cellphone in my pocket and took off after her. My shoulder ached but I ignored it and pushed my wings harder. The lights on the Parkway building blinked in the distance.

***

I could see the figures waiting on the top of the building when we drew near. My heart pounded in my throat at the sight of Seth and Sam tied up near one corner of the roof with Alice and Brian on the other corner. Two Galdoni stood by each pair. I pushed a button on the cellphone and shoved it back in my pocket. We landed on the roof. I met Seth's gaze. His eyes were wide and filled with tears. He couldn't speak past the tape across his mouth.

"About time you got here," Steel growled.

"How's your arm?" I asked, tipping my head to indicate the cast. "Maybe your name should be twig instead of Steel."

He took a step toward me. The Galdoni with brown wings I recognized from Alice's party grabbed his arm. "Remember why we're here."

Steel's eyes narrowed. "Give us the girl and you can have your friends back."

"Why would you keep your word?" Ava demanded.

Steel shrugged. "I guess you caught me in a good mood."

"What do they want with Ava?" I asked, stalling for time.

"What makes you think they want just Ava?" Steel asked.

A small pop sounded. I winced when something struck me in the chest and looked down to see a dart protruding from my shirt. I stumbled back as numbness ran through my arms and legs.

"That's right," Steel said, a sneer crossing his face. "We have orders to kill you, and I wouldn't mind doing it while your friends watch."

Ava grabbed my arm, helping me stand. "Are you so afraid of one boy that you have to tranquilize him first?" she demanded.

"He knows I can snap him in two," I said, my words slurring from the effects of the dart.

Steel gave her a predatory smile. "We have one for you, too, doll."

She shrieked when a dart hit her shoulder. "Coward," she spat, tearing it out and throwing it on the ground.

"Coward." Steel's eyebrows lifted. "We'll see who the coward is when you arrive at our destination. Any chance you remember Mr. Samuelson?"

I had never seen such terror on Ava's face. Her skin paled and a shadow of something animal came into her eyes, something scared and backed into a corner, ready to lash out but unable.

"I won't go back," she said, shaking her head. "He'll never touch me again." She stumbled toward the edge of the roof. I lunged for her.

"Grab her, idiot!" Steel yelled at the nearest Galdoni. "She can't fly with the tranquilizer."

Ava fell off the building. The tip of her gray wings vanished over the side as she plummeted. I jumped after her. My wings wouldn't work. I held them to my sides to fall faster. I reached Ava and pulled her against my body. I turned as we fell so I could shield her from the impact. Ava's eyes were closed. It was as if she had already accepted the fall as a better fate than returning to Mr. Samuelson.

I hit a pile of cardboard boxes and garbage that had piled up in the alley. Pain surged at the impact and I blacked out.

I forced my way back to consciousness, fighting the darkness with every ounce of strength I had left. I couldn't catch my breath. I couldn't feel my arms or legs. I forced my eyes open. Ava was on her knees. She kept repeating my name, but her head drooped and it looked like she could barely keep her eyes open.

Hands grabbed Ava's shoulders. "Let me go!" she shrieked. She bared her teeth and hit Steel like I had taught her, a punch to the face and a knee to the groin, except she was too slow from the effects of the tranquilizer. Steel slapped her hands away and gripped her in a bear hug. The effects of the tranquilizer took full effect. Her head lulled forward and she stopped struggling.

Sirens sounded in the distance. Steel's eyes widened. He looked behind me. "We've got to go."

"What about him?" the Galdoni I couldn't see asked.

"Finish him," Steel said.

A shadow crossed my face. I gathered my strength. It took every ounce of effort to lift an arm above my head in an attempt to shield it. Something hit my arm with the force of a battering ram before it glanced off my head.

"Come on," Steel commanded.

Another Galdoni grabbed Ava. They raised their wings, blocking out the sight of the moon rising between the buildings. The sirens grew louder. Something warm dripped down the side of my face. I couldn't keep my eyes open.

A voice spoke. "Reece, Reece, where are you?"

The sound was muted and distant. I realized it was coming from the cellphone in my pocket. I couldn't get the arm that had been hit to respond. The fingers of my other arm twitched. I shrugged my shoulder and managed to flop it across my chest.

"Reece, answer me," Kale demanded, his voice tight.

I worked the phone from my pocket. It fell onto the ground. "Kale," I rasped.

"Reece, oh thank goodness," he exclaimed. "Where are you?"

"They took her, Kale." Tears burned in my eyes. I closed them. "I failed her."

"We're on the roof of the Parkway building," Kale said. "I had Saro's phone traced. That was smart of you to call."

"Seth, Alice," I slurred.

"Your friends are safe," Kale reassured me. "We got here before the Galdoni could hurt them. They flew off, cowards," he spat. Concern flooded his voice. "Where are you?"

The sirens reached the end of the alley. I let out a slow breath. The tranquilizer and the force of the fall made it hard to draw air into my lungs. I could feel my brain protesting the lack of oxygen. The sirens' song echoed along the walls.

I remembered standing on the roof with Skylar, wishing with all my might that I could chase the sirens and help rescue people the way Superman did. Now the sirens were coming for me. I would have laughed at the irony, but my will was gone, taken by the wings that had swept Ava from my side.

Chapter Twenty

I knew Ava was gone the second I awoke. The pain didn't matter; the fact that I couldn't catch my breath didn't matter. I had promised her she was safe. I had to make it right.

I sat up and Saro caught me. "Let me go," I gasped. "I have to save her."

"Not like this," he argued, gentleness in his voice. "You won't be any good to her like this."

"He'll hurt her," I protested, fighting his grip. My struggles barely moved the Galdoni. I gritted my teeth. "I can't let him touch her."

"You're going to hurt yourself," Saro said. "Calm down or Dr. Ray will put a sedative in your IV; then you'll be no help to anyone."

The sense of his words ate through my adrenaline. Pain filled my nerves, threatening to send me under again regardless of whether Dr. Ray was there to help or not. I struggled to breathe. I settled back on the bed. Each breath sent stabbing aches through my sides. I had to focus to draw air in deep enough.

Saro's voice was subdued when he spoke again. "Dr. Ray said you broke a bunch of ribs and fractured your wings in that fall, not to mention your arm." I glanced down at the bandages. "He had to stabilize the compound fracture of both bones with plates, but you're going to have to take it easy."

"I can't take it easy," I said, fighting for strength. "I've got to find Ava."

"We're working on that," Saro replied. He rubbed the back of his neck, then leaned forward with his elbows on his knees. "Reece, what happened on that building? All we know is what the police captured from your phone call. When we arrived, the Galdoni were already preparing to leave." His eyes met mine. "But I think your call saved your friends' lives. They were definitely planning to push them off the roof. We got there just in time."

"We shouldn't have left without you guys. I know that." Guilt filled me at my stupidity.

Saro shook his head. "We found the note Steel wrote you. I can't blame you for doing what you felt you had to in order to protect your friends."

"Would you have handled it differently?"

He hesitated, then said, "Probably not. I'm as hotheaded as you are."

I gave a small smile that I didn't feel. "What do I do, Saro?" I didn't care that I let the despair I felt show in my voice. I was lost, adrift. Ava was out there somewhere probably afraid and possibly being hurt by Mr. Samuelson, whoever he was. "I need to find her."

Saro nodded. "I know, Reece. I know. We're doing our best."

***

The next time I awoke, I peered through the groggy haze to see Koden sitting next to the bed. He had his dark red wings pulled up on either side of the chair, and he was looking at something in his hand. His curly blond hair hung in his eyes. When he looked up and saw that I was awake, the intensity in his blue gaze made him look far older than a child.

"Are you my babysitter?" I asked, trying to keep the bitterness out of my voice for his sake.

The smallest hint of a smile touched his mouth. He held up whatever he had been studying. I raised my good arm and accepted it, amazed at how much strength it took to perform even that simple act.

My stomach twisted at the sight of an angel worked from the aspen wood I had given him for taking pictures to surprise Ava. The angel's face was bare, its features left to the imagination. It had wings crafted down its back, but instead of a lamb like in the picture Koden had shown me, the angel was holding a little bird. It was a crude carving, but well done considering Koden's age. The part that struck me most was the wings. Koden had painted them blue. They were the only part of the angel that had color.

"How did you do this?" I asked. "It's beautiful." I tried to give it back, but he closed my hand around it. I looked at him for a moment. There was so much faith and trust in his gaze. No Galdoni child had ever looked like that at the Academy. I let out a painful breath. "I can't take this."

He pushed my arm back onto the bed with the angel still gripped in my hand. Satisfied, he sat back on the chair and drew his knees beneath his chin, wrapping his arms around them to hold them in place.

Whatever Dr. Ray had put in my IV began to take affect again. My eyelids closed and refused to open. I let out a sigh and slipped back into the darkness.

***

"Saro says you're a reluctant patient," Dr. Ray said. At my silence, he smiled. "Every Galdoni is. You're used to being ready to fight the next day." His smile left. "But you almost got yourself killed this time, Reece. If those boxes hadn't slowed your fall, you wouldn't be here. That's for certain." He held up the x-ray he had been studying. "As it is, between the fractures along your wings and your broken ribs, you really are going to have to take it easy."

I couldn't stay quiet any longer. "How am I supposed to do that, Doc?"

Something in my voice made him pause. His features softened. He sat down in the chair and pushed his glasses up on his nose. He was silent for a few minutes. I was almost asleep from the pain medications when he spoke. "I was the first one to talk to Ava after Saro saved the female Galdoni."

He sat back and crossed one knee over the other, then linked his fingers together around it. "Those girls went through so much more than any person should. Girls who have gone through what they did have a wall, a protection of sorts. They hide behind nothingness. It's like you talk to them, and nobody is there to respond."

He let out a slow breath. "They can get over it with time and love, and they usually do." He smiled. "Ava was different. As soon as she was brought to the Galdoni Center, she asked me when she could leave. I thought she was running away, which was understandable, but no, she said she was tired of being a victim and want to take charge of her own life."

"She did that well," I said softly.

Dr. Ray nodded. "Very well. I kept worrying she would break, that the memories of what she had gone through would tear her down. But she made it through." He glanced at me, a grateful smile on his lips. "I understand I have you to thank for that."

I thought of the nights holding Ava. Even though she thought I was a killer and hated what the Galdoni represented, she had needed me in the late hours of the night when the memories became too much. "She had night terrors." My voice was quiet. My arms ached to hold her. That pain was far worse than the throbbing from the break in my right arm and the fractures through my ribs and wings. I would suffer them gladly every day of my life if it meant holding Ava and being able to keep her safe again.

"She's strong," Dr. Ray told me. "If anyone can survive until Kale finds her, it's Ava. She's a fighter, like you." He rose and patted my shoulder. "Trust Kale, Reece. He is putting everything he can into finding her. He takes the weight of her capture on his shoulders and feels responsible for Ava, as he does for every Galdoni and human within our Center. If anyone can track her whereabouts, it's him. Have faith."

His last two words lingered when he left the room. I lifted my hand. The little angle Koden had carved sat on my palm, its head bowed as it watched over the little bird. I closed my hand, cupping the angel inside.

"Please," I prayed for the first time in my life. "Please protect her."

***

The room was empty the next time I awoke. I felt restless, like there was so much I should be doing, but no way to do it. I sat up gingerly. Every movement hurt, and the pain inhibited my ability to breathe. I had to sit still for several minutes willing my lungs to fill. It felt ridiculous being so helpless. I was a Galdoni. Galdoni were created to bleed, to fight, and to die. Well, I had already done the first two, and I refused to obey the last.

I slid the IV from my arm. A trickle of blood dripped down my elbow. I ignored it and searched for my clothes. Someone, probably Skylar, had washed them and left them sitting on the small cupboard in the corner. The trick was getting there.

I clenched my jaw and stood up slowly. My wings had been bound tightly to my back to prevent movement, but the weight of them pulled at my broken ribs. The pain was enough to make my knees weak and threaten to send me crashing to the floor. I gripped the edge of the bed hard, refusing to go down. The pain didn't own me. I shoved it to the back of my mind as I had been taught to do a thousand times.

I remembered watching my left arm be stabbed by the point of a dull knife, seeing the blood well from the wound and drip with a dark patter onto the sand. My left hand held a sword balanced in the air. If I let the pain from the knife win and the sword drop, the punishment was a severe beating. The same exercise happened with a hot coal on the back of one hand and a katana in the other. If either fell to the ground, the payment was harsh. Eventually we all learned to put the pain as secondary, or at least pretend long enough to pass the test.

I kept the image of the blood dripping down my arm in my mind. The pain of my wings and ribs dulled enough for me to think. I took one step, then another. It was a small victory to finally reach the cupboard. Raising my arm high enough to reach the clothes pulled at my ribs. I sucked in a breath and grabbed them. The shirt was going to be too much with the wing bindings. I let it drop to the ground and pulled on the pants. Bending hurt, but I had lived with pain most of my life. I undid the ties on the hospital gown and let it fall to the floor beside the shirt.

I leaned against the door frame. No one was in the hall at the late hour. I could have pressed a button to call for help, but nobody could give me the kind of help I needed. Instead, I eased slowly down the hall to the elevator. Tears of despair filled my eyes when I pushed the button. I stepped inside and for a second it felt like Ava was standing next to me, both of us nervous as we rode the box up. I refused to glance over and shatter the feeling. My heart couldn't take it.

I stumbled out onto the twelfth floor. The room was dark and empty. The door to the roof looked so far away. I had to feel fresh air against my face and remind myself that I was alive. I pushed through the room. My breath came in ragged gasps, but I couldn't take it any longer. I shoved the door open and made my way to the railing.

"Ava, where are you?" I yelled at the top of my lungs. I tasted blood. I pulled in a few ragged breaths. The horizon was dark, the stars emotionless eyes in the ebony blanket that cloaked the world. The world was so big. How was I to find her in it? I fell to my knees and put my forehead against the rough roof.

"Reece?"

I tipped my head at the sound of Kale's voice. He hurried to my side and knelt on the ground.

"I can't find her, Kale. I can't save her. What am I supposed to do?"

"We're searching everywhere," he said, despair in his own voice. "We're doing everything we can."

"For all I know, she needs me at this moment and I'm not there. She might be in pain, she might be dying," my voice cracked, "And I'm not there to protect her." I buried my face in my hands. "For all I know, this is her very last moment and I'm not there."

I punched the roof. The pain ricocheted through my chest to my wings. I did it again. I lifted my arm to do it a third time, but Kale caught my hand. I struggled against him. He pinned me down. Adrenaline flared through me, chasing away everything but a red fog of rage. I drove the elbow of my broken arm back against his ribs. When his grip loosened from the blow, I brought my left shoulder down and rolled, bowling him over with my momentum. I came up in a crouch with my hands up, ready to tear him apart.

"Reece, stop it!" Kale yelled. "You're going to hurt yourself."

"Too late," I replied grimly. I dove at him.

Kale stepped to the left and brought an elbow between my shoulder blades that drove me to my knees. He spun around behind me and wrapped an arm around my neck. I tried to elbow him again, but he was ready and looped his other arm through mine. Every movement brought pain from my wings that were pinned between us. I couldn't catch my breath. The rage dissipated as my instincts to survive surfaced. I gave up and stopped fighting.

Kale waited a minute to ensure I was done before he let me go.

I fell to my knees and he knelt beside me. "I have to find her," I wheezed. "I can't sit by and do nothing. What if they've hurt her?"

Chapter Twenty-one

Kale sat in silence with one hand on my shoulder and the other clasped in a fist on his lap. "We're going to find her," he said after a minute. There was a new tone to his voice; it was filled with determination and promise. "I'm going to make it happen," he said. He pulled me up to a standing position and ducked under my good arm.

I was vaguely aware that when we reached the elevator, he pressed the button for the eleventh floor. The guide inside the elevator labeled the eleventh floor as staff offices. I had never felt the need to visit them. When we reached the floor, the doors didn't open.

"Name?" a recorded voice asked.

"Kale," Kale replied.

"Welcome, Kale," the voice said in monotone. The door slid open.

I stared at the rows of offices and equipment. Weapons lined several glass-walled rooms on the right side, while the left was filled with men and Galdoni on computers even at the late hour. A 3D computer-generated map of the all surrounding cities glowed in several locations.

"Come on," Kale said, helping me down the hall.

"What is this?" I asked in amazement.

He smiled. "Operational headquarters. We still haven't found all the Galdoni from the Academy, and those we find are seldom in savory situations. It takes a lot of work to protect both the Galdoni and the populace."

He nodded at a young man with brown hair as we passed. "How are things going, Nikko?" he asked.

Nikko put a hand over his mouthpiece. "The situation in Nester's tense, but officer negotiations are working."

"Good to hear," Kale said, patting his shoulder on the way past. Nikko gave me a searching look, but continued talking into the headset he wore. I caught the words "mass suicide" and "stealth prevention tactics" as we walked by.

Kale led me to the office at the end and helped me to one of the chairs near the side wall. "I should probably have them bring a hospital bed in here," he said.

"Do and I'll jump out that window," I replied.

He nodded. "I figured as much. Just don't pass out on me." He picked up the wireless phone on his desk. "Andrews and Lem, to my office."

A police officer in civilian clothes with only his badge on his belt to signify him as such glanced at me when he came in. Lem followed close behind, his red hair disheveled and pale orange wings hanging as though he was on the edge of exhaustion. He nodded at me before collapsing into a seat in front of the desk.

"Looking a bit worse for the wear," Lem called over his shoulder.

"I was about to say the same to you," I replied.

He chuckled and turned his attention back to Kale.

"Lem, you and Reece have met. Officer Andrews, Reece is Ava's closest friend." The officer and I exchanged a nod before he took a seat next to Lem. Kale continued, "Reece's interest in Ava's safe recovery has spurred me to take drastic measures to ensure Ava's location is obtained as quickly as possible."

I sat up, my focus entirely on his words.

"As such, I need to personally question Veto and Hound," Kale concluded.

Lem and Officer Andrews exchanged a glance. "We've questioned them both relentlessly," the officer pointed out. "None of the Galdoni have budged an inch."

Kale nodded. "That's why I need to talk to them. Please arrange it with Officer Donaldson so that the Galdoni are in the holding rooms when I arrive at the station."

Officer Andrews nodded and left.

Kale turned to Lem. "I'll have the questioning open-air. As soon as we hear anything, I want you and Saro ready to investigate."

"I'm going," I said. Denial washed across Kale's face. Before he could argue, I met his gaze. "I'm going."

Kale had already proven on the roof that, given my shape, I was nowhere close to matching strength with him, yet I wasn't about to give in and he knew it. He gave an exasperated sigh. "Fine, but you're going in the SUV."

"Agreed," I replied.

He speared me with a look. "And you're staying in the SUV," he said.

I nodded. "As if I could do anything in this condition."

He shook his head and turned back to Lem. "Have Saro come listen; the three of you wear earpieces and be ready to leave at a moment's notice." He picked up the phone again. "Bear, have the surveillance SUV ready to go. We'll need it shortly. Let Goliath know I need him to be the driver."

"Got it," the big Galdoni replied.

Kale put an earpiece in his ear and tossed me one. He set his hand on a sensor next to a wall panel. The sensor beeped and the panel slid away so that a gaping hole to the outside appeared. He gave me a short nod before jumping out. His black wings filled with night, a ghost in the darkness as the panel slid closed behind him.

"Come on," Lem instructed.

He moved to helped me to my feet, but I shook my head and did it on my own. I followed him into the main room.

Several men, women, and Galdoni were already waiting near a black section with buttons and speakers on the wall.

"Can you hear me?" Kale asked. The sound came from both my earpiece and the speakers.

"Loud and clear," Nikko replied.

"This isn't going to be pretty," Kale said, his voice cold.

Goliath and Saro entered the room. Saro grabbed a chair and slid it over to me. "Sit," he said softly.

I knew better than to argue, and I couldn't deny that sitting was a lot better than falling over. He stood behind me with a hand on my shoulder and turned his attention to the radio.

We listened to Kale check in at the police station. I recognized Officer Donaldson's voice. Their footsteps echoed in the Kale's earpiece as they walked down the hall. "I've told the boys anything goes. They're not to call you off until you get the answers you need." His voice lowered. "Because the Galdoni jurisdiction is still up in the air, you have full control here. Let me know if there's anything you need."

"Thank you," Kale replied, his voice level.

A door opened, then shut.

"Missed me?" a gruff voice asked.

"You going to wish you never said that, Veto," Kale replied.

The sound of a fist striking flesh followed. A heavy clank echoed through the room.

"I have rights," Veto yelled.

"You lost your rights when you attacked Crosby High," Kale replied. Two more strikes followed, then a pause. Kale let out a loud breath as he followed through another punch.

"I'm handcuffed," Veto protested, his voice tight as though he was trying to control his emotions. "Where's the honor?"

"You don't deserve honor." Punch. "Because of you, a girl is missing and potentially hurt or dead." Punch. "If you don't tell me what I need to know, you'll leave this room in a body bag."

A scrape of metal on the tile floor followed. I could picture Kale pinning the gray-winged Galdoni against the wall. Struggling ensued. A body slammed heavily to the floor. A whimper sounded.

"Tell me where to find Samuelson," Kale growled. "If you don't, you'll be dead and Hound will tell me, so you lose twice." His breath sounded heavy in my earpiece. Everyone waited, frozen in place with their attention on the harsh breathing in the speakers.

"Okay," Veto finally gave in. "Mr. Samuelson is in a big house. There's security."

"Where?" Kale demanded.

Veto gave an address. The men and Galdoni around me jotted it down.

"Let's roll," Goliath commanded. Saro, Lem, and two other Galdoni I recognized from the Academy but didn't know in person prepared to leave. Goliath walked with me to the elevator. The other four Galdoni jumped out another panel that slid away to reveal an exit to the outside. I envied their easy flight.

Goliath shuffled from foot to foot as the elevator made its way down. "I hate these things," he muttered.

"Nothing like a little box to remind you of home," I replied.

He gave a deep chuckle that rumbled through the elevator. "Guess I didn't know what I was missing."

"Does it make you homesick?" I asked, throwing him a sideways look.

He grinned. "Not in the least."

We stepped out at the first floor. Bear nodded amiably as we passed the desk. "Take care, gentleman," the Galdoni growled.

"You, too, Tiny," Goliath replied.

When I glanced back, Bear had a huge grin on his face.

The surveillance SUV was waiting outside the front door. My heart raced at the thought that we were heading toward Ava. I climbed onto the front seat the other Galdoni had left open for me. It was comical to see four adult Galdoni squeezed into the double seats of the SUV. With their wings and huge shoulders, they looked like bird sardines. I figured it would be at the best interest of my general welfare not to comment.

We couldn't get there fast enough. My heart raced at the thought of finding Ava. Was she safe? Was she hurt? Was she afraid? The questions kept running through my mind as we raced along the midnight asphalt. Stars glittered outside the window, untouchable beacons that reminded us there were still places we couldn't fly. Perhaps Ava was looking at the same stars. I put a hand on the window. "Please let her be okay," I breathed.

The angel Koden had given me sat in my pocket. I took it out and gripped it tight, hoping beyond hope that she was alright.

"I'm at the house," Kale said into my earpiece.

Goliath pushed a button on the SUV's dashboard; Kale's voice filled the car. "Lights are on and guards are staked at the doors. Stop at the library parking lot a block from the address. It's good you're coming in the vehicle; less chance to alert them if they have surveillance on the sky."

Goliath pulled into the parking lot a few minutes later. Kale was waiting for us. I climbed out to hear his orders. The black-winged Galdoni's knuckles were bruised and he looked weary but determined. "Our goal is to find Samuelson and locate Ava."

The name Samuelson sent a surge of rage through me. I clenched my fists. Kale held up a hand. "Reece, you stay with Goliath in the SUV. We could be running into a trap and you definitely aren't in any shape for a fight." I wanted to go in so badly, to be the first one to Ava to ensure that she was alright. I needed to know more than I needed to breathe.

Kale put a hand on my shoulder. "We'll let you know how she is as soon as we find her," he promised.

I nodded and took my seat in the front of the vehicle. Goliath walked to the back. At the push of a button, the seats folded and moved to the back while a side panel rotated to reveal a computer and surveillance equipment. "Ready," Goliath said into the microphone.

Kale gave him a thumbs-up from the parking lot. The Galdoni disappeared into the darkness.

"This is the worst part," Goliath said quietly. At my glance, he let out a slow breath. "If Kale gets hurt or ambushed, I'm not there to help. Instead, I have to listen and hope they have it figured out."

"What's the point of surveillance, then?" I asked.

His massive brow furrowed. "We record everything that happens, every conversation, the locations of the Galdoni, and what occurs while they are inside. It protects us if there is ever an investigation, and gives us what we need for additional research into security threats against the Galdoni." His voice lowered. "But I still hate it."

I nodded in agreement. My hands itched to help as we listened to Kale lead the others around the back of the compound.

"Lem, take out one and two left, Saro, you've got right. Drake, Stag, rush the door," Kale said quietly. "Our goals are silence and speed. I would like to avoid alerting Samuelson's full security staff, but with his set-up, I'm not sure that's going to happen. Either way, we can handle it."

Lem gave a quiet chuckle. "We've got this."

"Let's move."

We listened to the guards be taken out with swift efficiency. An alarm sounded loud enough that we could hear it from the library. Kale didn't speak, but we heard him rush into the back doors Drake and Stag had barreled down. Gunshots followed. Two screams sounded. Footsteps and loud breathing could be heard through the speakers.

"Take the left wing," Kale commanded to someone.

I was gripping the arm of the chair so tight my hand ached. I had to focus to let go. Every muscle in my body was tense. I glanced back and saw Goliath staring at the computer as though he could see what was happening. His jaw was clenched and his fists were balled on the keyboard. The machine beeped in protest, but he didn't hear it.

"Samuelson." Kale's shout made me freeze.

"To whom do I have the honor?" a cold voice responded.

"Kale, leader of the Galdoni," Lem replied. "You should probably bow."

Goliath shook his head at the Galdoni's brash answer, but listened without speaking.

"Kale. You know, I've heard of you," Samuelson said, his tone dry and musing.

"Cut the crap," Kale replied.

225

Something was thrown across the room. Somebody yelled. It killed me not to know what was going on. I should have been there. Samuelson needed to pay for what he did.

Apparently, Kale thought the same way. "Tell me where Ava is before I break your neck," he growled in a voice that made the hair on the back of my neck stand up.

"This is about Ava?" Samuelson wheezed through a restricted throat.

"Tell me!" Kale yelled.

"Sh-she was worthless," Samuelson responded. "She was broken. I thought you were hiding her because she was pregnant, but she wasn't." His voice hardened. "She should have been. They promised me she was fertile and sound. Advantage Corp lied. I made her pay for that lie."

I felt Goliath's gaze. I couldn't breathe. Every sound over the intercom grated against my ears. I heard Kale's angry breathing, the moans of whatever guards lay closest to the room where they had found Samuelson, and the quiet hum of a car over the road near the library. My heartbeat wasn't among the sounds; my heart had stopped at Samuelson's words.

A roar tore from Kale; the sound of splintering wood sounded loud through my earpiece. "What did you do to her?" he yelled.

"Why does it matter?" Samuelson protested, his voice quivering as he gasped out the words. "She was worthless."

Kale's voice lowered into a steely calm. "She is young and innocent."

"Innocent," Samuelson snorted. Another crash followed. A scream sounded loud through the SUV.

"Tell me where she is if you value your life," Kale said.

"She was garbage," Samuelson replied with a sob. "So I took care of her like garbage. She was disposed of."

"Where?" The one word hung taut in the air, filled with all the venom and steel of Kale's anger. I could picture him with his hands clenched, Samuelson lying broken at his feet.

"There's a parking garage . . . in Denson . . . my company. . . demolition in the morning for the new mall. . . ."

"Reece, it's your call," Kale said quietly. "Do you want me to kill him or serve him to Officer Donaldson for justice?"

I wanted him dead. I wanted to kill him with my bare hands. Every cell in my body screamed for him to be throttled, but even that wouldn't be the kind of death the man deserved after what he had done to Ava.

"Will a man pay for what he does to a Galdoni?" I asked Goliath quietly.

Everyone on the other end of the intercom waited in heated silence.

Goliath hesitated. A mixture of emotions crossed his face. He finally shook his head. "The Galdoni's place in society isn't solid enough for an answer."

The blood would be on Kale's hands. If I was there, Samuelson would already be dead. As it was, Kale was waiting for my orders to kill a man in my name, but the death would be his to carry out.

"A gun!" someone shouted.

Two gunshots rang out. A scuffle followed. Someone screamed, then silence.

"What happened?" Goliath yelled, his deep voice echoing through the intercom.

"H-he had a gun," Saro replied. He took several calming breaths. "Kale doesn't need your answer, Reece. Samuelson's dead."

Chapter Twenty-two

I threw my earpiece down. "Where's Denson?"

Goliath stared at me. "Reece, you're not supposed to—"

"Show me Denson, now," I demanded.

Goliath pulled it up on the computer. The city was about fifteen miles west of our location. He narrowed in on the location. The image was old, but it showed the parking garage toward the northwest end where construction on the mall had already begun.

"It'll take twice the time getting there by vehicle," Goliath said, "But I think in your condition—"

I threw open the door. "Take off my bandages."

Goliath didn't speak as he removed the gauze from my wings.

I forced them to open. The pain that flooded from the swollen joints about sent me to my knees. I put a hand against the door and willed the pain to the back of my mind.

"You sure you can make it?" Goliath asked.

"I'm sure," I replied.

Goliath climbed out of the SUV. "I'm going with you."

I forced my wings down and rose into the air. Every movement hurt. Goliath turned his tan wings west. I followed in his wake, using the updraft to conserve energy as we flew toward Denson. Ava was about to be killed. My heart pounded with her name. I had to save her. She deserved to live.

"You okay?" Goliath called over his shoulder.

"Great," I forced out.

"This all worth it for a girl?" he asked.

I stared at his massive wings. "You kidding?"

"Of course," Goliath replied. "I'm just trying to keep you from thinking about your pain. Any life is worth it. I've just never been in love." He looked back at me. "But I'd be afraid to face you with that look in your eyes."

"You need a girlfriend," I said, fighting to keep in the air.

Goliath shrugged. "I have a cat."

I couldn't help the small laugh that escaped me despite the situation. "A cat?"

"A kitten, really," Goliath said. "His name is Mr. Timmons. I found him by the garbage bins and Kale said I could keep him."

I smiled. "I'd keep him a secret. It might damage your reputation."

Goliath laughed. "As if I need to be more intimidating."

"True," I admitted.

Goliath pointed. "There it is."

His talking had distracted me enough that we had made it. Gratitude for the Galdoni's kindness filled me. He angled toward the parking garage and I followed. The extra pressure on my wings stole my breath.

"We have trouble," Goliath said.

Four Galdoni rose in the weak dawn light that filtered through the clouds. I grimaced. All four were the same Galdoni I had fought outside of Alice's house.

"That garage could be blown at any time. It sounded like Samuelson already expected it, so we don't have much time," Goliath called over his shoulder.

"I'll search the garage if you can keep them distracted."

"Will do," he replied.

"Watch out for Steel," I told the big Galdoni.

He glanced back. "He's a friend of yours?"

"Something like that. There are a few issues to settle."

Goliath grinned and popped his knuckles. "I like settling issues." He tucked his wings and dove straight at the group.

I followed close behind him. At the last second, I forced my right wing to raise and pushed the left one low. I spun to the side and cut through the group before they could stop me. I glanced back to see one Galdoni break free. The rest attacked Goliath. I dove through the lowest level of the parking garage, following my instincts which said Samuelson would do his best to bury his evidence completely. Nobody was in sight. A ramp lowered from the level I was on. I ran to it and my heart fell when I saw that the garage continued underground.

A hiss of wind warned me. I ducked in time to avoid Steel's attempt to ram me into the wall. He tucked his black wings and rolled, rising graceful into a fighter's stance near the ramp.

"Going somewhere?" he asked.

"Let me save her, Steel. Her death does not need to be on your head," I told him.

He laughed. "As if one more death matters." His eyes narrowed. "Of course, you were too young for the Arena. Maybe you don't know the victory of slaying your enemy."

"She's not your enemy," I pointed out. "She never hurt anyone."

Steel raised his arm. The cast was dull and dirty. "I wouldn't have this if it wasn't for her."

"She had nothing to do with that!" I protested. "I broke your arm. It's what you deserve for attacking students at a party."

He took several steps toward me, reiterating the thought that I probably should learn to control my mouth.

"She deserves to die as much as you do," he spat. "She failed to produce a child. That was the sole reason for her creation. You are a weakling and a coward, both attributes entirely against the meaning of our existence."

"I broke your arm, so what does that make you?" I replied before I could stop myself. I backed down the ramp, stalling for time as I searched for Ava. Steel jumped in front of me, blocking my path. I searched for words. "What I mean to say is, in nature, the ability to adapt is the key to survival for any species. Our world has changed, Steel. We need to be more than just bloodthirsty killers."

"Do we?" he asked with his predatory smile. "It's working out just fine for me."

He lunged. I dove off the ramp to the next level. When I spun around, Steel was there. He punched me in the chest, then slammed a haymaker into my jaw. I fell to the cement floor gasping. He tried to kick me in the stomach, but I caught his leg and rolled toward it. His knee gave a loud snap and he yelled. I pulled up to my feet using the wall.

Rage turned Steel's face red. He ran at me like a bull, using his wings to supplement his knee. I rolled backwards over the wall and fell to the next level.

The pain when I hit tore through me without mercy. I fell to my knees.

"You think you're clever?" Steel asked, landing gracefully on the ramp. "You think you can keep running?" He laughed and waved a hand to indicate the cement walls around us. "This place is coming down at any moment. Each level has been wired, so if you're not light on your feet, you'll be smashed as flat as that girl you're after."

"Where is she?" I demanded, using the adrenaline that surged through my veins at the thought of her in trouble to force myself back to my feet.

"You're getting closer," Steel replied. "Maybe we should just let you die together."

He dove at me. I drove an elbow against his head the same time that his punch caught me in the ribs. I fought for air. He shoved me against the wall to the next ramp. The force of my wings striking cement made spots dance in my vision. I used the wall to brace me against his next attack and kicked high. My foot caught him on the chin, snapping his head back. He stumbled sideways clutching his jaw. I pushed off from the wall and kicked again, using my aching wings to help me turn. The kick caught him on the side of the head. He fell to his knees. I used the wall to stay up.

"You will die with her," he growled. He rushed me faster than I could get my limbs to respond. His momentum bowled us over the short wall down to the next level. The force of the landing broke us apart. I lay wheezing, trying to pull in a breath to clear my darkening vision. I glanced to the side. A lone car sat in the middle of the floor. There were no more ramps. We had reached the bottom.

Strong hands closed around my throat. "I should have killed you the first time I met you," Steel glared down at me. "It's time for you to die."

I couldn't force Steel's hands away. My heart pounded loud inside my ears. I struggled for breath. Darkness pressed against my mind. I thought of Ava inside the car; hurt, maybe dying. If I died, she wouldn't make it out of the parking complex. I was her only chance to survive. I slipped my hand in my pocket and gripped Koden's angel. The sculpted blue wings bit into my hand. I pulled the angel out and slammed it into Steel's face.

He reared back with a yell, the angel protruding from his right eye. I jumped to my feet and bowled him over. He rolled beneath me, throwing me onto my back.

"Look what you did!" he screamed, leering down at me with blood dripping from his damaged eye.

My good arm was pinned beneath me. The one that had been broken throbbed from his weight pressed against it. I gritted my teeth and pulled it free.

"It's your time to die, Steel," I growled. I drove the heel of my palm against the angel sticking from his eye. I felt his skull give. I rolled, knocking his good arm out from under him. His face slammed against the ground, driving the angel completely in. His body shuddered, then grew still.

Before I could take a solid breath, explosions sounded. The detonation had begun. I pushed to my feet and ran toward the car.

"Ava!" I yelled. I threw the back door open. She wasn't inside. The door on the other side was also open. I ran around, my heart pounding. She was nowhere to be seen. The floor rumbled. I could hear the levels crashing above, one on top of the other. It wouldn't be long before the weight was too much and the underground levels were completely obliterated. I doubted they would dig them up. They probably just planned to build the mall right over the top.

"Ava, say something!" I screamed.

"Reece?"

The words were weak, a mere whisper amid the thunder that rumbled through the building. I ran forward. Pain, fear, darkness, everything fell away at the sight of Ava curled in the corner.

She didn't move when I touched her. I picked her up and ran toward the ramp. I used my wings the best I could to run faster. Pillars began to fall. The entire right side of the parking garage slanted down. I staggered and had to fight to remain upright as the ground shook and fell away. I pushed my wings hard, propelling us up the next ramp. One more and daylight would be visible.

The ramp collapsed in front of us. I clutched Ava tight to my chest as five stories of cement slid down. The roof above us cracked. There was nowhere to go. We were trapped. I hunched over Ava, shielding her with my arms and wings.

"Reece!"

Hands grabbed my shoulders and beneath my arms. I was lifted into the air with Ava held close. We broke through to the first floor. I glanced up to see Goliath on one side and Kale on the other. Saro flew in front, guiding us through the dust and falling debris.

"This way!" he shouted.

We flew out into the fresh air. The parking garage buckled behind us, sending up clouds of rubble. We landed on the grass nearby. I fell to my knees with Ava in my arms.

"Ava, Ava, talk to me."

Her head lolled back. There were bruises around her eyes and dried blood from a split along her lip. I could see tear tracks in the dirt that covered her cheeks. Her beautiful gray wings hung limp in my arms, dusty from the debris. A sob tore from my throat. "Ava, answer me," I begged.

A raindrop fell on my head. I looked past the Galdoni who surrounded me to the clouds beyond. The sunrise was obscured behind them.

I pulled Ava close and rose.

"Reece, what are you doing?" Kale asked.

"The sun," I replied. "She needs to see the sun."

I pushed my wings down, but they weren't strong enough to help me rise into the air with Ava in my arms. Gentle hands cupped my elbows. As if following an unspoken agreement, Kale and Saro lifted their wings. They carried me up to the clouds. Goliath and Lem followed, protecting us in case any of Steel's Galdoni decided to attack.

I could see the sunlight fighting to get through to the world below. The thought of the warm, healing light filled me with strength. "I'm alright," I told Saro and Kale. I lifted my wings. They ached, but I barely felt them. I rose through the last of the clouds. The darkness fell away, and we were basked in sunlight.

"Ava," I whispered.

It was beautiful. The clouds rolled like ocean waves blanketed in gold and edged in soft hues of rose. The sun felt like the warmest blanket around my shoulders. I turned slowly so that Ava could feel the sunlight on her face.

"Ava," I said again.

My heart skipped a beat when her head lifted. "Reece?" she whispered without opening her eyes.

"I'm here," I replied. Tears slid down her cheeks. I held her close. "You're safe, Ava. Samuelson is gone forever. He will never bother you again; I promise."

Her eyes opened and she looked at me. Her sea green eyes filled with sunlight. "I love you," she said softly.

My heart skipped a beat. "I love you, Ava, my angel. You are everything to me, and I almost lost you. Never again," I vowed. "You're safe and I won't ever let anything hurt you again."

"I'll fight them like you taught me," she said, her voice growing stronger.

I smiled down at her. "Ordinary school girl by day, fierce, feisty Galdoni by night. If anyone's Superman, it's you," I said.

She lifted a hand to my cheek. I turned my face into her palm and closed my eyes, letting myself feel that she was alright, that she was safe, that I had saved her.

"Reece." I opened my eyes with a smile at the soft way she said my name.

235

Her warm smile made my heart pound. "You'll always be my Superman," she said quietly.

I held her close. The warmth of the sun reminded us that a new day had dawned. The possibilities were endless, and the world was spread out beneath our wings.

"Should we go see Dr. Ray?" Kale asked from behind me.

Ava and I looked at each other. Her smile touched her eyes. "Definitely," I replied.

Even Superman deserves a break once in a while.

*** If you loved this book, please review it online so that so that others can find it as well! Keep an eye out for book 4 which will be here soon!

About the Author

Cheree Alsop is the mother of a beautiful, talented daughter and amazing twin sons who fill every day with joy and laughter. She is married to her best friend, Michael, the light of her life and her soulmate who shares her dreams and inspires her by reading the first drafts and adding depth to the stories. Cheree is currently working as an independent author and mother. She enjoys reading, riding her motorcycle on warm nights, and playing with her twins while planning her next book. She is also a bass player for their rock band, Alien Landslide.

Cheree and Michael live in Utah where they rock out, enjoy the outdoors, plan great adventures, and never stop dreaming.

Check out Cheree's other books at www.chereealsop.com

A Quick Thank You

I just want to say thank you to the many people who helped make this book possible. Thank you to my husband for patiently reading each draft, for finding plot holes, and for adding depth to scenes and helping them come alive. I couldn't do this without you!

Thank you to my children, my beautiful daughter Myree and my twin sons Ashton and Aiden. Your adventures, laughter, and love fill every corner of my life. I love every moment I'm with you. You are truly amazing and can accomplish anything you put your mind to. Thank you for your patience while I write, and for only destroying one computer in the process (the result of a sippy cup disaster). I hope someday you will lose yourself within these pages and fall in love with the world of your mother's imagination.

Thank you to those who have read drafts and given me valuable feedback, as well as catching as many typos as possible (and I apologize for those mistakes that still managed to sneak their way through). Thank you to Sue Player for your editing and your feedback. Thank you to Andrew Hair for designing the beautiful cover; it always comes back far more amazing than I ever could have imagined.

Thank you to my family for being patient with my runaway imagination and lapses into the world of fiction. I love you!

Thank you most of all to my readers. I am so grateful for your time, for your reviews, and for the emails I receive. I used to escape into books when I was younger and I always wanted to give the same escape back to others. I hope you found Galdoni 3: Out of Darkness and the Galdoni Series enjoyable and heartfelt. This was written for you.

With love, Cheree.

Printed in Poland
by Amazon Fulfillment
Poland Sp. z o.o., Wrocław

58457522R00137